Dragon Lost

Also From Donna Grant

Don't miss these other spellbinding novels!

Dark Warrior Series
Midnight's Master
Midnight's Lover
Midnight's Seduction
Midnight's Warrior
Midnight's Kiss
Midnight's Captive
Midnight's Temptation
Midnight's Promise
Midnight's Surrender (novella)

Dark Sword Series
Dangerous Highlander
Forbidden Highlander
Wicked Highlander
Untamed Highlander
Shadow Highlander
Darkest Highlander

Rogues of Scotland Series
The Craving
The Hunger
The Tempted
The Seduced

Chiasson Series
Wild Fever
Wild Dream
Wild Need
Wild Flame

LaRue Series
Moon Kissed
Moon Thrall
Moon Bound
Moon Struck

Dragon Lost

A Dark Kings Novella

By Donna Grant

1001 DARK NIGHTS

PRESS

Dragon Lost
A Dark Kings Novella
By Donna Grant

1001 Dark Nights
Copyright 2020 Donna Grant
ISBN: 978-1-970077-94-0

Foreword: Copyright 2014 M. J. Rose

Cover photo credit © Annie Ray/ Passion Pages

Published by 1001 Dark Nights Press, an imprint of Evil Eye Concepts,
Incorporated

Sign up for the 1001 Dark Nights Newsletter
and be entered to win a Tiffany Key necklace.

There's a contest every month!

Go to www.1001DarkNights.com to subscribe.

**As a bonus, all subscribers can download
FIVE FREE exclusive books!**

One Thousand and One Dark Nights

Once upon a time, in the future…

*I was a student fascinated with stories and learning.
I studied philosophy, poetry, history, the occult, and
the art and science of love and magic. I had a vast
library at my father's home and collected thousands
of volumes of fantastic tales.*

*I learned all about ancient races and bygone
times. About myths and legends and dreams of all
people through the millennium. And the more I read
the stronger my imagination grew until I discovered
that I was able to travel into the stories… to actually
become part of them.*

*I wish I could say that I listened to my teacher
and respected my gift, as I ought to have. If I had, I
would not be telling you this tale now.
But I was foolhardy and confused, showing off
with bravery.*

*One afternoon, curious about the myth of the
Arabian Nights, I traveled back to ancient Persia to
see for myself if it was true that every day Shahryar
(Persian: شهریار, "king") married a new virgin, and then
sent yesterday's wife to be beheaded. It was written
and I had read that by the time he met Scheherazade,
the vizier's daughter, he'd killed one thousand
women.*

Something went wrong with my efforts. I arrived in the midst of the story and somehow exchanged places with Scheherazade – a phenomena that had never occurred before and that still to this day, I cannot explain.

Now I am trapped in that ancient past. I have taken on Scheherazade's life and the only way I can protect myself and stay alive is to do what she did to protect herself and stay alive.

Every night the King calls for me and listens as I spin tales. And when the evening ends and dawn breaks, I stop at a point that leaves him breathless and yearning for more. And so the King spares my life for one more day, so that he might hear the rest of my dark tale.

As soon as I finish a story... I begin a new one... like the one that you, dear reader, have before you now.

Chapter One

Crete, Greece

The warm water slid over Annita's body as she dove into the crystal blue sea. It was a ritual she did every day without fail. The waters had called to her for as long as she could remember. Her parents hadn't been able to keep her out of the sea.

There were as many theories surrounding the waters around Crete as there were myths and legends about the ancient gods and goddesses. In fact, it was said that Zeus had been born in one of the caves on Crete. Annita didn't care about that, but she couldn't deny that without her daily swim, she didn't feel right.

Her strokes were strong as she glided through the water. Thankfully, she didn't have to fight the tourists for the beach since it was her family's land. Holdings that had been handed down for generations—and would pass to Annita's sister, Louiza, eventually. Annita wasn't upset about that. She had grown up in the house overlooking the Sea of Crete and its sparkling blue waters. Life had been idyllic, if not a little...odd.

In general, Greeks were a superstitious lot. How could they not be with all the tales of gods, goddesses, monsters, and heroes? Then there was the Seer in the family. Annita's great-aunt, Chara, had pointed to her and said, "She's the one."

For the longest time, Annita hadn't a clue as to what Chara had been talking about, and she hadn't asked her parents either. Until, one day when she was thirteen, she'd overheard their conversation and learned that she had a destiny of great importance—with a dragon.

Annita paused and treaded water as she turned in a circle to look back at her family's ancestral home. The villa was beautiful with its stark white exterior set against the vivid blue of the sky, the cobalt waters of the sea, and the vibrant plants of varying colors all around. She was descended from famous people, and her name was one known all around Crete and Greece. As a Dragoumis, she'd discovered early that her family was respected and revered.

And that respect continued with Chara. People from all over came to see her great-aunt, much as they used to do the Oracle in ancient times. To this day, Annita remembered feeling overwhelmed and shocked by what she overheard about her destiny. But she never got to talk to Chara about it because her great-aunt had died an hour later.

All Annita had was a memory of a conversation she wasn't supposed to hear. She hadn't known what to do with the information, and the fact that her parents didn't say anything to her left her reeling. For the next few months, Annita kept what she knew to herself until her grandmother stood on the beach, waiting for her one day after a swim.

Annita's gaze had moved to the rock Yaya had sat upon. That day had changed the course of Annita's life more than what Chara had told her parents. Just thinking about it brought a smile to Annita's face. She missed Yaya terribly. Her grandmother had been one of the strongest women she knew, but she had also been one of the kindest.

Lying on her back to float beneath the sun, she thought back to that day…

"How long will you go before you ask the question?" Yaya demanded.

Annita halted in the water as waves rolled past her onto the beach. "What question?"

"The one you're afraid to ask."

Yaya's dark eyes held her grandaughter's mercilessly. Annita wrung out her hair and walked the last few feet out of the water to sit next to her grandmother, then pulled her legs up to her chest and wrapped her arms around them.

"It's okay, γλυχιά μου, my sweet one. You're scared, as anyone would be."

Annita glanced at her grandmother. "Not you."

Yaya snorted loudly. "I'm afraid of a lot of things. The difference is that I don't let that fear control me."

"That sounds easier than I think it is."

"I never said it was easy," Yaya replied with a smile. She put her arm around Annita and pulled her close. "If anyone can do this, it's you. But there can't be a step forward without asking the question first."

Annita took a deep breath and swallowed. The question had rattled around in her mind for months, screaming to be let loose for her to gain answers. But fear had held her back. Until now. If Yaya thought she could do it, then she would. "What did Chara mean when she said my destiny was the dragon?"

Yaya leaned her head against Annita's and looked out at the sea. "My sister has always had the gift of seeing into the future of others. She spoke about things none of us understood from the time she began putting words into sentences. Chara's gift was something she didn't want at first. She fought it with everything she had, and it nearly ruined her life. Finally, one day, I found her on this very spot crying as she screamed to the heavens, demanding to know why this was her life."

"What happened?" Annita asked.

"Nothing. As you'd expect. I didn't say anything to her. Instead, I sat with her much like we're sitting now. She cried, and I held her. A long time passed before her tears dried. She told me that she had two options. She could make the things she saw in her mind go away forever by taking her own life. Or, she could embrace her gift wholeheartedly. She feared the latter more than taking her own life."

Annita frowned. "Why?"

"Because there is power in the Sight. She had seen things she didn't want to see, and she knew that would continue. There would also be others who tried to use her. I told her to follow her heart, and that whatever she decided, I would support. I told her I didn't want to lose my sister. I promised her that I would help her carry whatever burdens she had. We made a pact that day. And I've kept my part of it."

"Is that why you're here now?"

Yaya lifted her head and smoothed away a wet strand of hair from Annita's face with a smile. "No, γλυκιά μου, my sweet one. I'm here because you need guidance, and I can help you. You've asked the question, and I will answer it. First, let me say that Chara knew of your birth years before your parents had you. She also knew you would be the greatest of our line."

"I don't want to be great."

"Sometimes, that's out of our hands," Yaya stated with a shrug. "The truth is that, one day, you will find a dragon."

Annita shook her head. "But dragons aren't real."

Yaya simply smiled, an expression filled with patience, love, and wisdom. "Oh, but they are. Very real. They used to live on this island."

"What? I've never heard of that."

"Just because you've never heard of it doesn't mean it isn't true," Yaya cautioned.

Annita nodded, accepting that as truth. "What am I to do with this…dragon?"

Yaya pulled her close once more. "That, γλυκιά μου, is something only you will *know."*

"You mean Chara didn't tell you?" How could Annita get a part of an answer, but not the rest? This wasn't fair at all.

"She saw what she saw. Chara told your parents the same thing she told me, which is what I just shared with you."

Annita rolled her eyes, feeling more annoyed and frustrated by the moment. *"Did Chara say when this would happen?"*

"No. It could happen tomorrow, or when you're eighty. But it will happen."

Annita had replayed that conversation in her head many times in the following years. No matter how many different ways she asked Yaya the questions, she got the same answers. On the day her beloved grandmother passed, Yaya had held Annita's hand and reminded her not to let fear rule her.

That had been six years ago. And there wasn't a day that Annita came for a swim that she didn't look at the rock where they'd had their conversation and think of Yaya. Yaya had certainly left her mark on the world and on all those she loved.

Annita flipped onto her stomach and dove beneath the water to continue her swim. She had explored various caves around the island, including many surrounding her family's property. While it was nice to remain below water for long lengths of time thanks to the oxygen tanks, she still preferred to swim on her own.

There were several routes she took. Today, she opted for the longest distance to head to her favorite cave. Annita cut through the water swiftly, navigating the currents and rocks easily. Finally, she reached the outcropping. She stopped and smiled up at the large opening of the cave.

People often asked if they could dive the cave, but her father's answer had always been no. No one but the family swam or dove the caves. It was how it had always been, and it was how it would remain.

Annita had entered the cave in different ways over the years, but her favorite was with her head above water using the breaststroke. She was able to see the play of light reflecting off the pool and shining upon the ceiling of the cavern. The bright turquoise water and white sand were spectacular, but the real treat was the cave itself.

The opening led one to believe the space within would be large, and while it was, it was just the beginning. The cave continued with another opening above the water. Annita swam to the edge of the rock and pulled herself up. She sat there for a moment and closed her eyes, letting the calm of the place settle around her.

At sixteen, she and her older sister had spent an entire day exploring the cave. It went on and on, opening to caverns of different sizes until it ended in the largest one of them all. Annita had wanted to stay and explore, but her sister hadn't liked it and wanted to leave. Since no one had known where they were, they'd returned to the house.

But Annita had returned on her own often after that. Sometimes, she explored at her leisure. Other times, she remained in the main entrance, listening to the water lap at the rocks. No matter how hard she looked, she found nothing. But she couldn't stop the inner voice that kept urging her to search again. After all, Chara had said that she'd find a dragon, and Chara had never been wrong.

As old as Crete was, Annita believed that she would find some artifact from the past. She still held out hope. Maybe it would be today.

She smiled to herself and let one leg dangle in the water. Maybe it was the fact that her sister was now married with a child of her own, but Annita couldn't stop thinking about the prophecy Chara had told her parents. In all the years since the declaration, neither her mother nor father had said anything to Annita about it. The one time she'd mentioned it, her parents had quickly changed the subject.

Her mind cleared, and Annita found herself drifting off to sleep. She was in that strange realm between wakefulness and sleep where she could've sworn she heard Yaya say her name. It was the urgency in her grandmother's voice that snapped her eyes open.

She remained still, listening to the cave around her for several minutes. Slowly, she sat up and looked into the water, but there was nothing there. Still, she pulled her foot out just in case. Then, she looked around the cave. The moment she glanced at the opening, she stood and faced it. Her head tilted to the side as she peered into the darkness.

Something was different today. She didn't know what, only that it was.

Annita took a tentative step toward the cave, fear taking root. She stopped and squared her shoulders. She knew these caves like the back of her hand, just as she knew the waters around her home. There was no reason for her to be afraid.

"Fear doesn't rule me," she told herself and started walking.

Within five steps, darkness reigned. She paused long enough to search for one of the flashlights she'd stored throughout the cave. She flicked it on and held it up so it shone ahead of her. The deeper she walked, the more unsettled she became, almost as if she could sense something was about to happen.

Annita's heart pounded against her chest, but she kept walking, pausing to check each cavern until she reached the last one. Right before she looked inside, she had the insane urge to turn around and run as fast as she could back to the water.

Instead, she held steady and imagined that Yaya would've smiled at her. With that, she took one step into the cavern, then another. And another. On the fourth step, she stumbled to a halt when the light fell upon a large, beige head. Her heart felt as if it fell to her feet when the animal opened its eyes and zeroed in on her. Then it lifted its long neck, the head swinging toward her as it climbed to its feet.

Annita could hardly believe what she was staring at. A dragon.

Before that fact could even register in her mind, the beast was gone. In its place stood a man so stunningly handsome, so mind-bogglingly perfect that she thought she might be going insane. She caught a glimpse of a naked body with hard muscles. But just like that, it was gone, too, replaced by clothes suddenly appearing on his body.

"Who are you?" she demanded.

He raised a brow the same deep red as his hair as bright blue eyes stared at her. "I was about to ask you the same thing."

She parted her lips, trying to place his accent. He spoke impeccable Greek, but there was a hint of a brogue. However, she could care less about that. She had witnessed a dragon. *A dragon*! Just as Chara had predicted. Annita didn't know what to make of it. Or who he was.

While she tried to sort it all out in her mind, the man/dragon asked in English, "What are you doing in my cave, lass?"

Chapter Two

Royden couldn't believe the human had surprised him. He had arrived at the cave in the early morning hours, just as the sun came up. Having swum to reach the cave, he'd decided to rest for a few hours and soak up the fact that he was back in the land he'd once ruled.

What he hadn't expected was the arrival of a mortal—nor her beauty. And damn, was she beautiful. Tall, with large breasts outlined by her two-piece bathing suit, dark hair drying into waves from her swim, and a golden glow to her skin as if she'd been kissed by the sun.

Her pale brown eyes were mesmerizing as she stared. She had been startled to see him, but it hadn't been fear that he saw when she realized he was a dragon. He'd shifted to his human form quickly, hoping the small beam of her flashlight hadn't highlighted too much of him. But even his shifting and clothing himself using magic hadn't seemed to upset her. It was almost as if she had…known he was there.

And damn if he didn't want to discover more about her.

There wasn't time, however. Royden had snuck away from Dreagan for this quick errand without telling anyone. He'd intended to be back at the manor in Scotland before anyone was any wiser. If only the human had stayed away, he could've searched the cave as he wanted, then left at nightfall to start his journey home.

"Who are you?" she repeated, this time with authority in her voice.

Royden didn't want to like her, but he did. It took serious courage to stand up to a stranger in a cave, much less one who had used magic. He'd probably have to get Guy to come and wipe the mortal's memory of him. So much for no one at Dreagan knowing he was gone. Shite. This wasn't turning out as he'd hoped.

He threw her question back at her. "Who are you?"

"Annita Dragoumis. This is my family's land, and you're trespassing."

There was something about her bossy tone that went straight to his cock. Which was the last thing he needed. "I willna be long. I just need a few hours."

"For what?"

He sighed, doing his best to keep his patience. "I'm looking for something."

"Sure you are. The fact remains that you aren't supposed to be here."

Royden was finished playing games. He knew he was in for a world of problems now that a mortal hadn't just seen him in dragon form but had also seen him shift. He needed to turn the tables on her and quickly.

"You're in a dark cave with a man you doona know, and you're issuing demands?"

Her eyes narrowed. "You aren't Greek."

"No' in the least," he stated.

For a heartbeat, she stared at him as if trying to figure out his accent. "Welsh?"

"Now that stings, lass." Though he was impressed that she knew English.

"Scottish," she said with a smile. "You're from Scotland."

Royden bowed his head. "Now that we've gotten that out of the way, it's time for you to leave and forget you've seen me."

Annita shook her head of dark brown hair. "I can't do that."

She wasn't afraid to speak her mind or stand up to an unknown man in a cave, and she could speak fluent English. Who was this woman?

Royden shifted as his balls tightened. "You doona have a choice."

"I'm not so sure about that." She made a sound in the back of her throat. "You see, my great-aunt was a Seer, and she foresaw something of my destiny."

Royden stilled. All he could hope for was that the great-aunt hadn't seen him in this cave. Because if she had, then there was a good chance the woman had known Annita would find him.

Annita smiled, nodding. "That's right. She foretold I'd find a dragon. That I'd find you."

"I'm no' a dragon."

"I know what I saw."

He took a step toward her. "Do you now, lass? It was dark. That torch you're carrying doesna have a long beam of light. You could've fallen and hit your head, which addled you."

"I was meant to find a dragon, and I did. You. I didn't fall, and my head is not addled."

Royden could push things and see if he could frighten the mortal, but he found he didn't want to do that. If only he could get her to run away in fear. Isn't that what humans generally did at the sight of them? Why was Annita different?

"You don't know what to do with me," she said.

Royden ran a hand down his face. "Leave. Please."

"No."

"What do you want from me?"

Annita shrugged. "I don't know."

He raised his brows in surprise. "It was foretold you'd find a dragon, but you don't know what to do with one?"

"I thought you weren't a dragon," she replied with a grin.

Royden blew out a breath and looked away. He usually had no problem talking his way out of a situation. What the hell was wrong with him? It couldn't be just the pretty face staring at him? No, he had to admit the truth. It was the fact that he was back home after eons of being away. This was the very cavern where he and his brother had played as younglings. It's why he was here now. Long, long ago, his brother had buried a claw from their grandfather in this cavern. Royden was here to find it. He wanted that one memento of his life that the Others—a group of Druids and Fae who had combined their magic to fight the Dragon Kings—couldn't take from him.

He looked at Annita, noting her almond-shaped eyes and full lips set in her oval face. "Why have you no' run away?"

"This is my home."

"The cave?"

She rolled her eyes. "This land and the house upon it. Why should I run?"

"Because I could do you harm."

She thought about that for a moment and shrugged. "Harm could come to anyone at any time."

"While that might be true, lass, people doona usually stick around to find out. If they feel a situation is dangerous, they get out."

"I don't feel this is dangerous."

He gave a bark of laughter. "I find that hard to believe."

"Me, too," she answered with a frown.

They stared at each other for a moment. Royden knew he should find a way to either make her leave or depart himself, but once again, he didn't want to. He was baffled by his predicament, but at the same time, he was enjoying it. It was quite the conundrum.

"I'm Royden," he told her.

Her lips turned up in a smile. "Now that we know each other's names, perhaps you can tell me what it is you seek. I might be able to help you."

"I thought you wanted me gone."

She looked away for a moment, shrugging. "Yeah. I am supposed to want that."

"It's okay to change your mind."

"And you? Have you changed your mind about wanting me to leave?"

Royden chuckled and nodded. "I do think that might be the case."

Annita turned away, biting her lip. She walked a few paces, then stopped and looked at him. "I think I'm a pretty good judge of character, and I don't feel as if I'm in danger with you. That could be because I'm not, or maybe I'm in more danger than I've ever been in my life. Which is it?"

"You want me to answer? What if I'm lying?"

Her brows lifted briefly. "I don't know."

Royden backed up a few steps. "I'll tell you this, if I wanted to silence you, I could've done it before you even knew I was in the cavern."

"Why didn't you?"

"I hoped you'd turn around and leave."

"And when I didn't?" she pressed. "You could've left without me knowing, right? Why didn't you do that?"

He blew out a long breath. "You think I could just disappear?"

"Since it seems as if you've just appeared, yes."

This was where Royden should lie about who and what he really was and what he could do. He'd lied so many times before to keep the secret of the Dragon Kings. What was one more lie to one more mortal?

It shouldn't be anything, but somehow, it was.

"Why did my great-aunt Chara know I was going to find you?" Annita continued. "Despite her being a Seer, she didn't know more. Or if she did, she never shared it. Do you know why I was meant to see you?"

Royden shook his head. "Nay, I can no' say that I do."

"Interesting." She sat on a boulder and tapped the flashlight against her leg, making the beam of light bounce across the floor and wall. Her pale brown orbs lifted to his. "I don't suppose you'll tell me who you are."

"I did."

"Not your name, but *you*. Are you a dragon, or are you a man? Or are you both?"

Royden rubbed a hand over his mouth. "You have a lot of questions."

"I know I saw you as a dragon, and then you changed to…this," she said, motioning to his body with her hand. "If you can do that, then I think you could do pretty much anything. Disappearing so I couldn't see you or…" She trailed off. "Or maybe you can't disappear. Is that why you shifted? Hoping that I didn't see you as a dragon? If that's the case, then no wonder you've been pressing me to leave."

He frowned, unsure of where to start answering—or even if he should.

"Maybe you know you *should* make me leave or even hurt me if I don't. Perhaps you don't want to. Is that it? I hope that's it. Because, otherwise, I'm not sure what we're doing here."

Royden blinked. The woman had a slew of questions, and most times she answered them herself. Which left him wondering what it was he should answer.

Annita gave him a pointed look. "Well?"

"Well, what? You said a lot."

"I suppose," she replied with a shrug. "Can you disappear?"

"No' in the way you think."

She gave a slow nod. "Are you going to hurt me?"

"No' if I doona have to."

"Hmm. Not what I was hoping to hear."

He bit back a smile. Her commentary was humorous. Most people kept those things to themselves, but not Annita.

"Are you a dragon or a man? Or both?"

Royden looked away. He hadn't lied to her yet, and now that the opportunity presented itself, he found he couldn't. She had seen him. He'd had the chance to shift before she came into the cavern, and he hadn't. Why? He'd been asking himself that from the moment the torchlight fell upon him.

The survival of the Dragon Kings depended on the mortals not knowing of their existence. There were a select few humans not mated to a King who knew about them, but it was rare. And with the Others out to destroy them, the Kings had to be extra careful.

"It's okay," Annita said. "You don't have to tell me."

His silence was answer enough. They both knew that. He might not have defined who he was, but she had seen him. He'd *allowed* her to see him. That was the most perplexing part of all.

"I've always loved this cave," Annita said into the silence. "Ever since the first time I discovered it. I come here often. My sister and I explored every inch of this one day long ago. She didn't like the dark, but there's something about this place that makes me feel safe."

"That's what it's meant to do."

She cocked her head to the side. "Oh?"

He looked around, thinking back to when he was a youngling, long before he was a Dragon King and ruling his clan. "Many beings use caves as homes."

"This was your home?" she said, her eyes brightening. "Of course. It's large enough for you, not that I got to see all of you. I just caught a glimpse. But you've come to look for something," she said, changing the subject. "I'd like to help. If you'll allow me."

"The best thing you can do is leave and forget me."

"That's not going to happen." She made a sound and shook her head. "I've known for years that I was going to find a dragon. Part of me thought it might be a toy dragon or some relic from my ancestors, but Yaya knew it would be a real beast. She knew it would be you. I'm meant to see you, and that couldn't have happened for me to just forget. Wouldn't you agree?"

"I'm no' sure I'm in a place to make those kinds of decisions."

"Are you not in command of your life? Shouldn't you be able to make those choices?"

Royden chuckled. She certainly had a way of putting things. "Aye. I'm in charge of my own destiny."

"I keep talking, trying to learn more about you to determine if I should be afraid of you, but the longer I'm with you, the more comfortable I feel. With a dragon. How strange is that?"

"Strange," he agreed.

She briefly looked at the ground. "Can you change back so I can see you better?"

He nearly did as she asked before he realized the folly of her request. Royden was conflicted. He wanted to talk to Annita, to let her see him in his true form, and answer all of her questions. What harm could one mortal do?

But he knew all too well what one human female could do. While he didn't believe that Annita would start another war between the dragons and humans, Royden simply couldn't take the chance.

He walked to her until only a foot separated them. With a smile, he said, "You're special, Annita. I've never met another like you."

"I've never met anyone like you," she replied.

He had the insane urge to reach up and touch her cheek. Instead, he used his magic and let loose a flash of light, blinding her. With her attention diverted, Royden made her fall unconscious. He caught her in his arms as her flashlight fell from her fingers and flickered off as it rolled away.

Royden held Annita for several minutes before he carried her back to the water. He laid her on the rocks. Just before he straightened, he let the backs of his fingers caress down her cheek.

"Farewell, sweet Annita. When you wake, you'll realize you were sleeping. This was all a dream. Nothing more," he said, pushing magic into her so his words penetrated her mind.

Royden hoped it worked. He didn't want to call Guy in to wipe her memories. After gazing at Annita for another few moments, Royden rose and stalked back to the cavern to begin his search.

Chapter Three

A sigh of contentment fell from Annita's lips as she came awake slowly. The sound of the water coming in contact with the rocks in the cave was soothing. So soothing, in fact, she was often lulled to sleep as she clearly had been today.

Some might say she didn't have a direction in life. That wasn't true at all. Not only did she help handle the running of the estate, but Annita also *liked* a simple life. Yes, she lived off the rewards of her ancestors, but she'd never spent lavishly. She drove the same vehicle she'd gotten ten years ago, and she was just fine with that.

She yawned and stretched her arms over her head as she looked at the ceiling above her and the reflection of the water that danced upon it. Most times, when she came to this cave, she found it difficult to leave. Maybe it was because of the prophecy about her finding a dragon, but... Her mind trailed off as she recalled doing just that. Had it been a dream? The image of the beige dragon was seared into her mind, more real than anything she knew. No fantasy had ever given her anything so...tangible before.

But...if she had seen the dragon, what was she doing here?

Annita sat up and looked toward the tunnel leading farther into the cave. For a moment, she could've sworn she had deja vu. She swallowed and stared into the darkness. Annita searched her mind, but all she could remember was seeing the dragon.

No. Wait. She closed her eyes and relaxed as an image of something slipped away before it could form. Instead of seeking what it was, she listened to the water to calm her mind. It wasn't long before a man took shape in her memories. A very handsome, alluring man with thick red hair and bright blue eyes. One who smiled at her. Her stomach quivered in response.

No dream had ever made her do that. Regardless, if she had seen the dragon who turned into a man, she wouldn't have left him. She would've stayed and spoken with him.

Annita didn't know what to think at the moment. She couldn't be sure what was real and what was a dream. The fact that she'd just woken and thought of the dragon could be a sign. It wouldn't be the first time she'd opened her eyes to believe she was still very much in a dream. Yet, there was something different about this one. If anyone had asked her, she would've staked her life on the fact that Royden had been real.

Royden.

She jerked as his name went through her mind. There was no way she'd just made up a name like that. Did that mean it hadn't been a dream?

"Or perhaps one so vivid I believed it to be real," she murmured to herself.

Annita looked at the dark tunnel again. For the first time, she didn't want to go down it. Not because she was afraid, but because she didn't want to traverse it and not find Royden waiting for her.

She could recall every inch of his face from his strong jaw and thin lips to his penetrating gaze. It all had held her transfixed. And his voice. Just thinking of that deep Scottish brogue made her close her eyes in ecstasy. How could she remember things with such detail if they had not been real?

Without a doubt, she knew she wouldn't be able to. Not on her own, anyway. And while she should've been on guard, she didn't feel any fear. That in itself made her believe that it was a dream because there's no way she would've spoken so easily with a man who was trespassing on her family property.

It was too bad he hadn't been real. He was gorgeous.

Annita rolled her eyes at herself. Dragons weren't real. She didn't care what Chara or Yaya said. The prophecy that she'd find a dragon didn't mean an actual real-life dragon that could barely fit in the cavern. It meant a toy dragon or something with a dragon on it.

Besides the fact that dragons weren't real, Annita was fairly certain that if Chara and Yaya believed it would be an actual dragon, they would've prepared her more. No doubt it was all some elaborate hoax.

The minute that thought went through her head, Annita knew it was a lie. Chara might have been many things, but she wasn't a liar. Her abilities as a Seer were proven. It was just too bad Annita hadn't had a chance to talk to Chara herself and hear exactly what her great-aunt had told her parents. Listening through a wall had muffled many of the words.

All these years, she had never told her parents that she knew, and they had never spoken of it to her. Perhaps it was time for Annita to rectify that.

With that decision made, she jumped into the water and began the swim back to the estate. This time, Annita didn't stop. By the time she reached the beach, she was breathing hard. She walked from the water and wrung out her hair before she grabbed the towel and dried herself. Annita looked at the house as she put on her robe and slipped her feet into her sandals to make the trek back.

As she reached the steps, she could hear her mother's voice. It was a one-sided conversation, which meant her mother was on the phone. Annita ascended the stairs and came to the deck area where her mother, Selini, sat beneath the umbrella at the table drinking a coffee. As soon as she saw Annita, her mother waved her over.

Annita smiled in thanks to the maid, who handed her a glass of water. Once seated, she looked out over the sea, but her gaze was drawn in the direction of the cave. Soon, she was absorbed in thoughts of Royden.

The touch of something on her arm jerked her attention to the present. Annita looked over to find her mother staring at her, a brow raised in question.

"Are you all right?" her mother asked. "You seemed a million miles away."

Annita shrugged. "Just thinking."

"Is it about your sister inheriting the estate?"

Everyone had been asking about that, and it didn't seem to matter how many times Annita told them that she didn't care. No one believed her. "I promise, it isn't that."

"Even if it is, this will always be your home. Your father's sister lived here for years until she decided to move out."

Annita tried to be patient. She'd heard all of this before. Many, many times. "I know. Please hear me when I tell you that isn't what's bothering me. Nor is it the fact that my sister is married and has a child."

"I'm very aware," Selini said with a sigh. "I was hoping you'd be married by now with a child of your own. This house is large enough for many grandchildren to be running around."

"The estate is big enough, but I'm not sure about all of us living together."

Her mother waved away her words. "It's how it's done in your father's family. You know that. Chara and Yaya lived here for their entire lives. Just as your father and I will. And you and your sister."

"I don't think I will." The statement came out of nowhere. Annita had never had that thought before, so she was as shocked as her mother when the words fell from her lips.

"Annita, what's going on?" Concern filled her mother's brown eyes. "You love this place."

Annita nodded, looking at the water. "I do. More than you can imagine."

"Then why did you say that about leaving?"

Annita shrugged and returned her attention to her mother. "I don't know. It just came out."

Her mother searched her face for a long, silent moment. "Louiza never stops talking to me. She tells me things I'd rather not know. You, on the other hand, have always kept so much to yourself."

"Not because I didn't want to share them with you."

"You can share them now."

Annita drew in a breath and crossed one leg over the other. "All right. I know about the prophecy about me."

Selini blinked before her gaze slid out to the sea. "Chara wasn't supposed to tell you."

"She didn't. I overheard her telling you and Dad. Well, I heard some of it."

"Then you spoke with Yaya," her mother guessed.

Annita nodded. "I did. She confirmed what Chara had seen in her vision."

Selini took a drink of coffee and softly set the cup back on the table. Then her gaze turned to Annita. "I know how truthful Chara's words are. She predicted that I would get pregnant four times, but only have two children, both daughters. That was before I even met your father. She and Yaya were in the village and saw me. Chara walked over and told me all of that. I didn't know what to say because most people paid handsomely to get information like that, yet I hadn't gone to Chara. She came to me."

"And look at you and Dad," Annita said with a smile. "You've had a good marriage."

"Yes, we certainly have."

Her mother fell silent, and Annita looked down at her hands in her lap. This might be all she got from her mother, and if it was, then she would go to her father. It was time she knew everything.

"Chara told me that one of my daughters would do great things," her mother said suddenly. "For so many years, that's all she would tell me or your father, no matter how much we pressed. After a while, I thought that's all Chara knew. I learned later that she'd kept her secret for a long time."

Annita stared at her mother, waiting for her to continue.

"Both you and your sister did well in school. Both of you were not only beautiful but also intelligent. Both of you loved the estate and were eager to be a part of things. I didn't care which of you did great things. I just wanted you and Louiza to be happy. The year your sister turned sixteen, Chara told us her predictions were about you." Her mother chuckled as she shook her head and smoothed her shirt. "I told Chara that was nice, but in my opinion, both of my girls were going to be great."

Annita grinned. "I take it Chara didn't agree?"

"Not in the least. She took my and your father's hands and told us the entire vision."

"Which is?" Annita pressed.

Her mother licked her lips. "What do you know?"

"Only that I'm to find a dragon. That's all I overheard, and that's all Yaya told me."

"There's more."

Annita frowned. "Why have you kept it from me? And why didn't you want Chara to tell me?"

"You're my flesh and blood," her mother said, reaching over and covering her hand with hers.

"And I always will be."

Her mother turned her head away and dropped her hand back into her lap. "Chara saw you find a dragon—a beige beast."

Annita's heart skipped a beat. "What did you say?"

"A beige dragon."

"A real dragon?"

Her mother shrugged. "Chara only said a dragon. I didn't bother to ask if it was real or not because dragons aren't real."

Annita nodded. "Right."

"Anyway, Chara said that after you found this dragon, you'd be shown two paths. You'd have to choose one."

Annita rubbed her forehead as the start of a headache began. "That makes no sense. How am I to do great things if I don't know which path to take?"

"I asked the same thing. Chara said the dragon and danger go hand-in-hand. I knew that if you learned of this, you'd go around looking for the dragon, thinking it was some adventure. I didn't want you in any danger, so your father and I decided not to tell you."

Annita leaned her head back against the chair. "Both of you should know by now that what Chara sees comes to pass, regardless. She didn't tell you what age any of this would happen, did she?"

"Unfortunately, no. A mother doesn't hear that her child will be in danger and not think her baby might get hurt and die. I wanted to know how and when to protect you."

Annita leaned forward and put her hands on her mother's arms. "Chara would never have told you that if she knew I would die."

"You can't know that. Chara saw life, death, and everything in between. And she didn't hesitate to share what she saw. Sometimes, she left the death part out because she knew it would cause that person to alter their lives. Chara believed when your time was up, it was up, and nothing should interfere with that—not even a Seer."

Annita slowly sat back with this new knowledge. Her thoughts took her back to her conversation with Yaya on the beach. "Why dragons? Everyone knows they aren't real, and yet Yaya told me that they used to live right here on our land."

Her mother shrugged and reached for her coffee. "I don't know. But you're right, there is no such thing as a dragon. If there were, the world would know. Nothing stays secret any longer. It hasn't for a very long time."

"Yeah. There's no such thing as dragons," Annita said and thought back to her dream of the beige dragon that'd shifted to a man.

Or was it a dream?

Chapter Four

He'd done the right thing about the mortal. At least, that's what Royden kept telling himself. Why then was he still at the cave? He should've been on his way back to Dreagan by now. Instead, he'd remained behind, half hoping that Annita would walk down the tunnel again.

"Shite," he mumbled to himself as he leaned his head back against the wall of the cave.

While she'd slept, he'd searched for the item buried by his brother. At one time, Royden had been furious with his brother for hiding it. Royden had then stopped looking for it, and it wasn't long after that he became King of Beiges. He'd soon forgotten about the talon. It wasn't until the war with the humans that Royden even thought about it again. However, by then, it was too late.

He blew out a breath and rubbed his eyes with his thumb and forefinger. The damn thing was in this cavern. Of that, he was sure. But he hadn't found it yet. The problem was that he didn't know if he was really looking for it or not. The fact that he kept thinking about Annita and debating going to check on her while she slept told him that his attention wasn't where it needed to be.

When Annita had finally woken, he'd remained hidden in the shadows, watching her. He knew the moment she thought about finding him. Royden had held his breath, wondering what she would do. Nothing was stronger than dragon magic. He wasn't worried about Annita remembering everything. But when she frowned and looked down the tunnel to where he hid, he began to wonder if she just might shake off his magic. In the end, however, she'd slipped back into the water and swum away.

It was for the best. Now that he was alone, Royden could really look for the talon. Why then was he standing in the same spot, wondering what Annita was doing?

He had to stop thinking about her. She was a distraction he didn't need. The last place he should be was in Crete, and yet he remained. He couldn't for the life of him figure out why he wasn't on his way back to Dreagan, especially when his brethren needed him. Constantine might have returned to Dreagan, but there was still so much up in the air. It was the reason Royden had taken the time to make this trip.

Royden walked through the tunnel, letting his fingers glide along the rock. How many times had he and his brother rushed through here, running after each other? He'd never thought of leaving the area. The warm waters, the bright sun, it had been paradise to him. But Fate had something else in store for him—to be a Dragon King.

It had come as a surprise, but he had accepted his path. In fact, he'd rejoiced in it. Royden hadn't realized how much until he started leading his clan. That's when he'd found his true calling. He loved being a Dragon King—even when things went bad.

He stopped when he reached the back cavern. With his enhanced eyesight, he could see the claw marks his brother and he had left on the rock. They were high up from where they had played. The gouges weren't easily seen by mortals in the dark, but with the proper lighting Annita—or anyone who ventured here—would be able to see them.

There was a push as Con's voice filled his mind. *"Royden."*

"Aye?" All dragons spoke through a mental link. The fact that Con had reached out told Royden that his absence had been noted.

"Is everything all right?"

Royden hesitated. He wasn't sure how to answer.

"You can tell me," Con urged.

Royden blew out a breath. *"I'm no' in Scotland."*

"I'm aware."

Two words, but they said so much. Con not only knew where Royden was, but he also most likely knew why. Yet Con was giving him a chance to speak for himself. One of the many reasons Con was King of Dragon Kings.

"I should've told you," Royden began.

"I just want to know if you're okay."

"*I doona know.*"

There was a pause before Con said, "*Fair enough. Do you need anything?*"

"*Nay. I'll return soon. I'd planned to already be on my way back.*"

"*But?*" Con pressed.

"*I've no' found what I'm looking for.*" Or had he? Royden's thoughts immediately shifted to Annita.

Con blew out a breath. "*I wouldna have stopped you from going.*"

"*I know.*"

"*But I wish you would've brought someone with you.*"

"*I needed some time by myself.*"

Con said, "*I can appreciate that. This mess we're in isna something that will be over quickly or finished neatly.*"

"*Is that why you knew where I was?*"

"*Aye. Do what you need, but keep in contact with me. And watch yourself.*"

Royden briefly closed his eyes. "*I will. You have my word.*"

Con severed the link. Royden was shocked that Con hadn't demanded that he return home. After all, things were really beginning to heat up with their enemies. For so long, the Dragon Kings had ruled this realm, but now, it was being threatened. There was a good chance they might have met the ones who could push them out. And that didn't bode well for the mortals who called this planet home.

Once more, Royden thought of Annita. He wished his mind didn't continually turn to her, but there was something about her that drew him. Was it the fact that she hadn't been afraid of him? Or was it because she'd said it had been prophesied that she would find a dragon?

Both things intrigued him in a way that worried him. He wanted the answers, and in order to get them, he had to remain in Crete. The longer he stayed, the more he would have to worry about enemies. For all he knew, Annita was a foe.

"Nay," he murmured.

He didn't know why he was so sure that she wasn't, but he was. Maybe it was the way she had looked at him with such awe and wonder. Perhaps it was how she had tempted him with her smile. It could be a million different things. Unfortunately for him, he'd never been one to stop digging for answers when he wanted to know something. And he really wanted to know about the prophecy.

He couldn't do that while in the cave, however. That meant it was time for him to venture out. Unlike some Kings, he didn't hold a grudge against the humans. He didn't mind being among them. In fact, he'd had many of them as lovers throughout the long years since the war.

His cock began to harden as he imagined what it would be like to have Annita as a lover. Her tiny bathing suit had left little to his imagination, but he wanted nothing more than to rip the material from her body so he could feast his eyes upon her. Then he'd lick her all over, teasing her nipples before settling between her thighs and lapping at her clit until she was shaking with need.

Only then would he fill her.

Royden drew in a shuddering breath and gave himself a shake. He couldn't let his thoughts linger there, not now. He might have come looking for something from the past, but it was a mortal in the present that now fully occupied his thoughts.

He returned to the tunnel but veered to the left into a smaller cavern. There, he moved aside a large boulder that blocked an entrance and jumped into the water. He returned the rock to its place with magic and dove deep so that no one would see him as he swam to shore well past the boundaries of the estate.

Once on land, Royden replaced his sodden clothes with dry ones with merely a thought. He made his way up to the street, looking first one way and then the other before deciding to go right. He walked for miles, simply enjoying the climate. It made him think of the long-ago days when dragons ruled. Before the mortals.

With a smile, Royden paused next to a shop that rented Vespa scooters. In minutes, he was driving one down to the village. It had been a long time since he'd smiled so freely. He knew a lot of it had to do with the fact that he'd returned to the place of his birth.

Most Kings kept away from their homelands since the memories that returned were hard to deal with most times. For the moment, Royden had nothing but happy thoughts. But memories of the war, of watching members of his clan and family die, of sending the dragons away, and the Dragon Kings going into hiding were always on the periphery.

However, he didn't let those memories in. Not yet. There would be time for that later. For now, he would enjoy his visit.

Royden parked the Vespa and leaned against it with his arms folded over his chest as he watched the comings and goings of the village. It didn't take long for others to notice him. The men eyed him warily, but the women were all smiles. He returned their grins and gave them a nod.

There were a fair number of tourists on the island as well, but they were easy to pick out. Since Royden needed locals, his observation quickly picked out the place he was searching for.

It was a small café where the locals got one menu, and the tourists another. The wait staff was friendly to everyone, but the locals got special items because they knew what to ask for. It was something done in a great many tourist towns.

Royden waited for a car to pass before he crossed the road and made his way to the café. He took a seat and waited for someone to come to his table. The waitress had sandy blond hair and a welcoming smile. He greeted her in Greek, and they shared a few pleasantries before she gave him a menu for the locals.

He ordered and continued watching others. It didn't take long for the food to come, but he took his time eating since others were sitting close to him. Eventually, they left. The next time the waitress walked past, he stopped her.

"What do you know of the family who lives in the grand estate on the beach?"

"The Dragoumis?" she asked, then shrugged. "Nice enough. Their family is one of the oldest in the area. They've lived in that house for generations."

Interesting. As was their surname. "Do you like them?"

She frowned. "That's an odd question."

"No' really."

"Why do you care?"

He shrugged one shoulder. "Just curious. I believe I met one of them today. Annita."

The waitress suddenly smiled. "I know Annita. She's very sweet. The whole family is, really. But she's the nicest of them all. If I didn't know her, I'd never believe she was from that kind of money."

"Oh?" he asked, quirking a brow.

"She doesn't flaunt it, if you know what I mean."

"I do."

She frowned at him. "You act like a local, but if you lived here, you'd know all about the Dragoumis family."

"I used to live here long ago. I'm getting reacquainted with everything."

"Ah," she said with a nod. "Is there anything else?"

"No' at the moment."

After she left, Royden finished his drink then laid down money to cover his bill and leave a nice tip. Then he rose and walked away. He wondered how long it would take for Annita to learn that he'd asked about her. That left him smiling as he made his way back to the Vespa and drove to a hotel.

Once he was in his room, he opened the double doors to the balcony and looked out over the sea, the same waters Annita had swum in not so long ago. His gaze slid toward her home. He could just make it out. He'd gone to a great deal of trouble to make her forget about him, but he was going to disrupt all of that by staying.

But how could he leave, knowing there was some prophecy? He had to get to the bottom of it. Anything involving dragons was something that needed to be investigated. Royden should've told Con. Although, to be fair, Royden had still been trying to talk himself into returning to Dreagan at the time.

He blew out a breath and said Con's name through their mental link.

"*Aye?*" Con answered.

"*I didna tell you everything,*" Royden said. "*When I was in one of the caves searching for something my brother hid long ago, a mortal found me.*"

"*When you say found you, do you mean—?*"

"*Aye,*" Royden answered. "*She saw me. I heard her coming and believed that she might pass me by. She didna. She saw me. And she saw me shift.*"

Con was quiet for a long moment. "*Is that why you're staying? Did she run screaming? Did others come for you?*"

"*Actually, she didna run at all. She told me that it had been foretold she'd find a dragon.*"

Con blew out a breath. "*I wasna expecting that.*"

"*Neither was I. She wasna sure what to make of me, but she was certain of the prophecy. I used magic to make her sleep so she would think she dreamed it all.*"

"*Did it no' work?*"

"*It did.*"

"*But you're still in Crete.*"

Royden chuckled softly. "*I am. There's something about this prophecy that bothers me. Especially with all we're dealing with right now. I need to see this through.*"

"*It could be a trap,*" Con cautioned.

"*I'll keep that in mind. But you know as well as I that we need to get to the bottom of this.*"

"And if she tells others about you?"

"We'll have a lot of cleanup to do."

Con made a sound at the back of his throat. *"Let me know if you need backup. One of us can be there in an instant."*

"You have my word."

Chapter Five

No matter what Annita did, she couldn't stop thinking about her dream. Although, she still wasn't certain it was a dream at all.

She looked at herself in the mirror, gazing into brown eyes that stared back at her. Her conversation with her mother the day before had netted her very little information. Not that she could call her mother a liar because the conviction her mother had while speaking on the subject of dragons was hard to dismiss.

Annita rolled her eyes. Dragons. Who in their right mind would be discussing dragons? No one. Because they weren't real.

She put her head in her hands and blew out a loud breath. She had even returned to the cavern earlier to look around. Just as she suspected, there wasn't anything that would make her think there had been anyone there—much less a massive dragon.

"I'm losing my mind," she murmured.

The sound of heels clicking on stone reached her through her closed door. Annita sighed as she heard her sister and her brother-in-law coming down the hall, headed toward dinner. The last thing Annita wanted was to join everyone. She didn't feel up to talking or carrying on any type of conversation. Not when she'd rather remain in her room, thinking about her dream.

A knock sounded on her door, jerking her head up. "Yes?" she called.

The handle turned, and the door cracked open to reveal her

mother. Selini smiled and cocked her head to the side. "Everything all right?"

"Yeah."

"You can say it isn't," her mother replied. "You don't have to please everyone."

Annita drew in a breath and swiveled on the vanity seat to face her mother. "It's what we do in this family. We please others."

"Oh. You're sassy tonight," she said with a laugh as she closed the door behind her and walked farther into the room.

"Maybe."

Her mother sat on the bed and regarded Annita for a few moments. "Your father and I have taught both you and your sister to have minds of your own. Yes, we do ask things of you in this family, but they aren't unreasonable."

"You're right. I'm sorry. I'm not myself tonight."

"This is about Chara's prophecy, isn't it?"

Annita licked her lips. "It is."

"I didn't figure what I told you yesterday would be enough." Her mother sighed and looked away. "I hoped it would, but I should've known better. Anytime Chara gave someone a prediction, the people she shared with tended to hold on to it."

"Like you did."

Selini's gaze slid back to Annita as she laughed, nodding. "Exactly."

"Is there something you aren't telling me?"

Her mother shrugged. "A lot, probably."

"About the prophecy."

"I told you all I knew."

"What about Dad? Does he know more?"

"Not that I'm aware, but you can ask him."

It was something Annita intended to do later.

"Cheer up, please," her mother urged. "I learned fifteen minutes ago that your father was bringing someone to dinner."

Annita leaned her head back and groaned loudly. "If he's trying to set me up on a date again, I'm not going down."

"We just want you to be happy."

She rolled her head to look at her mother. "I am happy. Why do I have to have a man for everyone to think I'm complete? I'm just fine the way I am."

Her mother threw up her hands. "I hear you. And as far as I know, no, this man isn't someone your father wants to set you up with."

"Dad doesn't bring just anyone home. Who is he?" Annita pressed.

"You'll learn like the rest of us. Now please come downstairs."

Annita stood and slipped on her red heels. She checked her appearance once more in the mirror before joining her mother and walking downstairs. One night every week, the family dressed for dinner. Which meant she couldn't go down in jeans or shorts.

When Annita had been little, she'd looked forward to those nights. Then came the time when she hadn't wanted to go down and resented her parents for making her. Now she found that she enjoyed it again. With how busy everyone was, it was the one night a week where they were all together. There were no electronics at the table to distract anyone. Just everyone catching up and talking.

And, occasionally, bickering.

They were a family, after all.

When they reached the main floor, Annita and her mother passed by her father's study. The door was cracked, and she spotted her father standing next to another man. He had his back to the door so Annita couldn't get a glimpse of him. But she did catch enough to notice that he sported a nice cut in his suit.

"I saw you looking," her mother said in a whisper.

Annita looked at her, and they both laughed before joining the rest of the family until dinner was called. Usually, her father and whatever friend or associate came to the house joined them, and they went to dinner together. Not so this time, which made Annita even more curious.

Before long, they made their way to the dining room. The smells coming from the kitchen were delicious and made Annita's stomach grumble in anticipation. She took her usual seat and was chatting with her brother-in-law when her father walked in.

He then stepped aside and held out his hand as his visitor came into the room. "Everyone, please let me introduce Royden Dreagan."

"Thank you all for allowing me to join you this evening," Royden said in Greek.

His gaze skimmed over Annita. She couldn't move, couldn't breathe. The man standing in the dining room was none other than the dragon she'd spoken to in her dream. Even his name was the same. She couldn't make something like that up.

Unless you're a Seer.

The moment the thought went through her mind, she dismissed it. She had no such gifts, and there was no use trying to say that she did to explain what had happened to her.

"Mr. Dreagan is from Scotland," her father announced with a wide smile. "He's here to look at buying a home."

Her mother smiled as her head swiveled to Royden. "Oh, how nice. This gives us time to practice our English."

Royden bowed his head. "I will speak whatever language you choose, ma'am."

"How did the two of you meet?" Annita asked. She waited until Royden looked at her before she turned her head to her father.

Emilios motioned for Royden to sit as he lowered himself into a chair. "I overheard him speaking to someone about a property. I pointed him to a few other places that he might like. Then we struck up a conversation."

Annita's heart was pounding so loudly she couldn't believe no one else heard it. She could feel Royden's gaze on her, but she refused to look at him. She wanted to jump up and demand to know what was going on, but she somehow remained in her seat.

The others took turns talking to Royden, asking him all sorts of questions like why had he chosen Crete, was he single, and how long was he staying. He answered them all with a smile on his face.

"Dreagan," her mother said with a frown. "You don't happen to be involved with the whisky company, Dreagan, are you?"

Royden gave a nod. "Actually, I am."

"That logo is very distinctive. Two dragons," her mother said and looked at Annita.

Annita wasn't much of a drinker, so she didn't know what was going on. But she heard the word *dragon*, and that was enough for her.

The conversation turned, but Annita kept that part to herself. Even her mother grew quieter after that. She didn't need to ask her mother to know that she was thinking about the prophecy and talk of dragons the past couple of days. Now, someone from Dreagan—a company that had dragons as their logo—was at their home?

The meal progressed slowly. Annita didn't taste anything. She smiled when someone said something funny, but otherwise, she didn't join in the conversation. No one seemed to notice, least of all her father, who seemed utterly enamored by Royden. Not that she could blame him. The man was charismatic…and absolutely gorgeous.

She'd seen him naked for a heartbeat, but even in his dark suit, he was breathtaking. Maybe because she knew what was under the material. Or because she knew he was really a dragon.

When the meal was finally finished and they'd moved into her father's study for drinks and more conversation, Annita was surprised to find Royden watching her. She raised a brow but otherwise said nothing. That only made his lips turn up in a grin.

After a while, she grew tired of listening to the conversation. She made her way to the balcony and stood beneath the moon and stars to watch the sea.

"This is a stunning view."

She'd known he would follow her. It was one of the reasons she had come outside. Annita didn't turn around to look at Royden. "It is."

He came up to the railing beside her. "If you'd rather be alone, I can return inside."

"I'd like the truth."

"What truth is that?"

She faced him and looked into his blue eyes that seemed to have a light within them. "The truth of who you are."

"Royden Dreagan."

"Are you going to stand there and tell me we didn't meet yesterday in the cavern?"

He studied her for a heartbeat. "You believe we met yesterday?"

"I know we did. On this property, in a cave. You can lie all you want, but I know what I saw and heard."

"And what was that?"

She took a step closer to him. "You were a dragon with beige scales, and you changed into...this," she said, gesturing to him and looking him up and down. "The next thing I knew, I woke up from what felt like a nap, thinking I had dreamed it all."

"But it wasn't a dream?" he asked.

"You know damn well it wasn't. You did something to me. What did you take from the cave?"

Royden glanced through the doors to the others. "Those are some bold statements."

"They're the truth. Why are you really here now?"

"You," he replied.

He hadn't actually said anything to confirm her words about the cave, so his admission now took her aback. "What?"

He chuckled. "I'm certain I had that same look on my face."

"So it was you?"

Instead of answering, he looked out at the sea. "There has always been magic in the moonlight."

Chapter Six

Royden hadn't expected that being so near to Annita would make him crave her. But that's exactly what it did. The surprise in her eyes when she first saw him alerted him that his magic hadn't relegated their meeting to a dream.

And, in a lot of ways, that made him happy.

He hadn't liked how she'd all but ignored him during the meal, however. He couldn't figure out if she didn't recognize him, was angry that he was here, or felt something else entirely. The first chance he got to speak with her, he took it.

She hadn't disappointed him.

Annita was spirited and unafraid to speak her mind—even to a dragon. She had no idea what he really was, but she wasn't afraid. It would be safer for her if she did have a healthy dose of fear, but he was glad she didn't.

"You haven't answered me," she stated.

He held back his grin and slid his eyes to her face. She was stunning. Her brown eyes were unmoving, her gaze unyielding as it held his, waiting for his answer. Her back seemed made of steel, her voice laced with determination. Ah, yes, she was spectacular.

And her body. The bathing suit had shown him her form, but the curve-hugging white and red dress left him aching to see more.

"Nay, I have no'."

She kept one hand on the railing. "What are you afraid of? My family learning the truth?"

"You don't know the truth."

"I asked. I'm waiting for an answer."

Royden smiled and licked his lips. "I doona think now is the right time."

"It's the only time."

"Or what?" he asked at her ultimatum. "You'll tell your parents what, exactly?"

Her nostrils flared as she realized that he was right. She faced the water once more. "Fine."

Royden watched her for a few moments. She was angry, and she had every right to be. However, he had to protect himself and his brethren. "Is that all you have to say to me?"

"If I were you, I'd leave. My patience is at its end."

"I thought you had more spunk than that."

That got her attention. Her head turned to him as she pierced him with a disapproving look. "If you want someone to pass the time with, the rest of my family will do. If you want to answer my questions and actually have a real conversation, then you can stay with me. You decide."

Damn. She was bossy. And he loved it.

"You're still here," she said with a sigh.

Royden chuckled. "I am."

"Are you going to talk?"

"I thought that's what we were doing."

She sighed loudly and glared at him once more. "Are you intentionally being obtuse? Or do you just like goading me?"

"My apologies," he said seriously. "I was teasing you, and that wasna fair. I've just no' run across someone like you before."

That made her frown. "I'm not sure how to take that."

"As a compliment. Most people doona keep me interested. However, with you, I'm hanging on each of your words. You doona back down, no matter what I say. I like that."

"Thank you?" She said it like a question, as if she weren't sure.

Royden smiled and said, "It was me in the cavern."

With those words, it seemed as if a great weight had been lifted from her. "Thank you."

"Initially, I didna intend to come here or talk to you. I was going to leave. But I couldna."

"Why?"

Royden glanced at the water and shifted his shoulders in his jacket. "This prophecy you spoke about."

"Oh."

Was that disappointment he heard in her voice? He was certain it was. He debated whether to tell her that *she* was also a reason he remained, but he thought better of it. As it was, he could hardly keep his hands to himself. If she looked at him as she had in the cave, he wouldn't be able to control his desire. It was better if she was angry at him or trying to keep her distance.

That would be better for both of them.

Are you sure?

Royden ignored his conscience and held Annita's gaze. "You didna run from me."

"I wasn't scared," she said in a low tone.

"You should've been."

"Why? Because you were a dragon?"

He gave a nod and took a half step closer to her. "Aye."

She briefly looked at the floor of the balcony and shrugged. "I was startled. Shocked. Amazed. But I had no fear, for some reason. Why did you let me see you?"

"I doona know."

"Are there others like you?"

He hesitated, not wanting to answer.

She waved away her words. "Forget that. It doesn't matter. Why did you come here?"

"I told you. I was looking for something."

"I can help."

He blew out a breath. "Thank you, but it isna in the cave. It should be, but it's gone now."

"How can you be sure?"

Royden grinned at her. "You know why."

"Right," she said with a smile. "Have you given up finding whatever it is?"

"I'll keep looking while I'm here."

"Maybe you were mistaken about the location."

"That isna possible. Those caves were our home. The one in the back was the place my brother and I used most often. He told me that's where it was hidden."

Annita leaned her head to the side, her soft brown locks moving with her. "What is it you search for?"

"Something distinctly...my kind."

"I don't understand."

Royden put his hands in his pants' pockets and shrugged. "It's from a dragon. My brother took it from me long ago and buried it."

"I see. Can you ask your brother where it is?"

"He's no longer here."

Annita's face crumpled. "I'm sorry for your loss."

He nodded and looked at the sea. "I heard that your family has lived here for many generations."

"We have."

"Have any of you done much exploring of the caves?"

She looked down at the water. "None of us recently, but I believe one of my ancestors did. Why? Do you think they might have found something?"

Royden shrugged as he looked her way. "Possibly. It would've been a relic. Something that would most likely fetch a fortune."

At his words, her face paled.

"What is it?" he pressed.

Annita glanced through the glass doors at the others and waved him after her as she moved down the balcony. They entered the house by another set of doors, and he followed her through the room, then down a long corridor and through a maze of halls until, finally, she opened a door and stepped inside.

Royden paused at the door as the lights flickered on. It looked like a storage room of sorts. He waited as Annita rummaged through some boxes until she pulled out a photo album and began leafing through it until she stopped and looked up at him.

"Is this what you're searching for?" she asked.

He took the old photo album with its yellowed pages and disintegrating black and white photos. His gaze looked at each of the pictures until he found the one she had indicated. It was of a man holding a drawing of a dragon claw. It was large, from an adult dragon. And just like that, Royden was taken back to his childhood. His grandfather had given him that claw as a present. It had belonged to one of the greatest Kings of Beiges that had ever ruled their clan.

Royden had kept it close, refusing to share it with his brother, who got jealous even though he had gotten something from their grandfather as well. To his brother, Royden's token was better, and he wanted it.

Like most siblings, they fought, especially over the claw. And then his brother stole it and hid it away.

It had created a rift between them that lasted for years. No matter how many times he demanded that his brother tell him where the claw was, he wouldn't. And Royden wouldn't go to his parents to make them force his sibling. No, it was between them.

His brother kept the secret until the day the dragons left the realm. Only then did he share the location with Royden. But Royden had other things to think about than coming to Crete to get something he'd lost long ago. Once more, he'd promptly forgotten about it. Until recently.

"One of my ancestors in the eleventh century supposedly found this," Annita said. "The family was doing okay financially, so it was kept hidden. It wasn't until the Dragoumis fell on hard times years later that another ancestor took it and sold it. The artifact fetched enough that the family was able to sustain themselves in lavish comfort. From then until now."

Royden slowly closed the album and handed it back to her. "Thank you for showing me."

"I'm sorry."

"Don't be," he told her. "What was left behind was for anyone to find and use. I can no' be angry about that."

She frowned, holding the album against her. "But it was yours."

"It was."

As soon as he admitted it, he saw the shrewdness come over her face.

Annita put away the photo album and faced him. "Either you're a very good liar, or you're very, very old, and have maintained yourself well."

Royden couldn't help himself, he laughed. "I'm no' a liar."

"It would've been easier if you were."

"Why?"

"Because now…" She trailed off and sighed. "Well, it means that now I've got to come to terms with the fact that you're much older than you look."

He raised his brows at her. "It's okay that I'm a dragon, but no' immortal?"

"Immortal?" she asked, her voice squeaking.

Royden instantly regretted his words. "I see that was a mistake to say."

"No, no," she said, shaking her head. She took a few steps back and put her hands on her hips. "You're right. I don't know why I'm acting like this. It's stupid."

"No' stupid," he told her.

She rolled her eyes. "It is."

"Why?" he prodded, wanting her to come to the realization herself.

Annita threw up her hands. "Because people aren't supposed to be immortal."

"And people are supposed to be dragons?"

"Well, no." She laughed. "I sound deranged. I blame it on the fact that I knew I was going to find a dragon."

He gave her a skeptical look. "Did you think it would be a real dragon, though?"

"I...honestly, I don't know. I think I was open to it."

"But magic and immortality are difficult to accept."

She wrinkled her nose. "For me, apparently it is. I'll get past it."

He shook his head at her. "You doona need to."

"I want to."

"Why?"

Annita smiled at him, her eyes crinkling. "Because I was supposed to find you."

"And what were you supposed to do after you found me?"

"That's a very good question," she said with a small laugh.

He frowned. "No one told you?"

She gave a shake of her head. "Nope."

"Interesting."

Annita moved to stand before him. "My great-aunt Chara was never wrong about what she saw. She didn't say when I'd find you, only that I would."

"What if I bring destruction to your family or you?"

Annita's brown gaze briefly moved to the floor before she shrugged. "Then you will. I think if that was supposed to happen, Chara would've told us. I know Yaya would've shared that with me."

"Chara might no' have seen it."

"I guess we'll never know."

Royden was in awe of her. "Does nothing scare you?"

"Everything scares me. I just don't let fear rule my life. I'm in charge. And if something scares me, then I do it anyway."

"What about people?"

She shrugged and tucked her hair behind her ear. "I listen to my instincts. There was nothing about you in dragon form or this one that told me I should be afraid."

"Maybe I'm the one who should be scared."

A slow smile pulled at her full lips. "Of me? A mortal?"

"Aye, lass."

"Hmm," she said in a husky timbre. "Isn't that interesting?"

Royden watched as she walked past him and out of the room. And damn if he didn't follow, wanting to verbally spar more with her. But more than that, he wanted to kiss her, to hold her, to spend the night showing her unspeakable passion that would leave them both breathless and wanting more.

Chapter Seven

Annita lay in bed, staring at her ceiling, her thoughts on Royden as dawn broke. She hadn't gotten much sleep the night before because she couldn't stop thinking about him. After she showed him the photo, they had returned to the others. Given the look her father gave her, he hadn't been at all upset that the two of them had gone off by themselves. Even her mother had smiled.

Royden had been affable and charming for the rest of the evening. He paid everyone the same attention, but Annita often felt his gaze on her. She fought not to look at him, not to think about what it might be like to have him as a lover, but it was a fight she couldn't win.

When he finally departed the night before, she thought he might give some indication that she would see him again, but she should've known better. Royden was nothing if not mysterious. He gave her a smile while his blue eyes held hers. The smile was different than those he'd given the rest of her family. Actually, it wasn't his smile. It was his eyes. In them was a multitude of secrets, and she'd only learned a couple. She wanted to know them all, and she thought he just might tell her.

She wasn't sure what that meant for her, and honestly, she didn't care. The need, the desire to know more about Royden was unavoidable. He was sinfully charming, mouthwateringly handsome, and uniquely different than anyone she'd ever met. Only a fool would turn away from such an opportunity.

Annita threw back the covers and rose to her feet. She walked to her window and looked out over the sea. Her gaze was drawn to the place where she'd first met Royden. It had been his home. The idea that he was a dragon and immortal was preposterous. At least it would be if she hadn't seen him with her own eyes. But she had. She knew the truth.

Though no one else would likely believe her.

That was fine. She didn't intend to tell anyone his secret. She wasn't sure how she was in on it, but she was happy that she was. A million questions still swirled in her mind. One of which was: *where were all the dragons?*

Just as she was about to turn away, she saw something in the water. Annita narrowed her eyes to get a better look. Then she smiled when she caught sight of the dragon. Royden was back.

She quickly changed into a bathing suit and rushed down to the beach. No one was up at this hour, and even if they were, no one would think it odd that she was swimming. Annita tossed down her towel and kicked off her shoes before running into the water until she was deep enough to dive.

In no time, she was at the cave. The moment she lifted her head from the water, she found Royden standing on the rocks, waiting for her. She smiled, her stomach fluttering oddly when he returned the non-verbal greeting.

"You're up early," he said as he helped her out of the water.

She shivered at the contact of his hand with hers. "I saw you."

"Did you?" he asked with a grin.

"I still didn't get a good look. I'd like to see you."

One red brow rose. "Would you, now?"

"Why do you sound surprised?"

He glanced down at their still-joined hands. "You've no' been afraid of me. I doona want that to change."

"It won't."

"You can no' predict that."

Annita moved closer to him, looking deep into his blue eyes. "Show me. Please."

He was quiet for nearly a full minute before he gave a nod and released her. Royden then took several steps back. "I willna harm you."

"I know," she said with a smile.

In the next instant, a dragon stood in his place. It happened in a blink. Annita leaned back her head to look up at him. She had known that he was big, but she hadn't truly understood just how massive he was until that moment. Now she realized why he'd thought she would be afraid.

Because she was. A little. How could she not be while facing a being of such proportions? She drew in a breath, realizing too late that she had held it. Annita blinked up at Royden as he stared at her with unblinking gold eyes. He blew out a soft breath, and she couldn't help but feel as if it were a sigh. As if he knew she was scared.

Annita wanted to kick herself. She'd assured him that she wouldn't be afraid, and yet that's exactly what she was. Instead of running as he expected her to, she let her gaze run over him. His scales were huge and glistened as if they were metallic. He was beige in color, but yet it looked like flecks of gold were in the scales as well.

Her gaze ran down his front limbs to see the long, dark cream talons. She squatted beside one and gently touched it. The claw alone was longer than her arm. This was what her ancestor had found and sold for a fortune. This was what Royden's brother had hidden from him.

She stood and lifted her face to him once more. He stood as still as stone, his gaze never leaving her. Annita took several steps back to get a better look at him, from the wings folded at his sides to the tail that had a stinger on the end of it. He was regal, majestic. And absolutely terrifying.

"Yaya would've loved to have seen you," she said.

Royden's large head cocked to the side. Then he shifted into human form, clothed once more. But he didn't come toward her.

Annita didn't take offense. She went to him instead. Smiling up at him, she said, "You're...more than I expected. I understand why you cautioned me."

"You wanted to run."

"No," she corrected. "I was taken aback by your size. I wasn't afraid you'd hurt me."

He looked at the water. "Maybe you should've run. It's no' good to be friends with one such as me."

"I disagree."

Royden snorted. "You doona know the truth."

"Then tell me."

His head jerked to her, his gaze narrowing. "You think that will make things easier for you? It willna. It will only make them worse."

"I'm not sure why it would make things worse. Royden, you're a dragon. You have magic. And you're immortal. I don't know why you don't tell the world."

"I forget sometimes," he said in a soft voice.

She frowned, not understanding him. "Forget what?"

"How naïve mortals are. And how you doona know the real history of your origins."

That sounded…ominous. Annita wasn't about to back down now, though. "Then tell me."

"I think no'. It was wrong of me to ever show you myself, much less stay. I knew better."

Before he could walk away, she stepped in front of him. "But you did stay. Why?"

His lips curved into a soft smile. "You. I stayed because of you."

That made her ridiculously happy. Too happy, in fact. She tried to warn herself not to get caught up in the emotions, but it was already too late. She didn't care that he was immortal and she mortal. She didn't care that he was a dragon and she only human. None of that mattered to her.

"I'm glad you stayed," she told him.

"You say that now."

"I will say that now and always."

He shook his head. "There is so much you doona know, Annita. If you had all the facts, you might no' so readily pledge such words."

"I know you. That's enough for me."

"It shouldna be."

"Then tell me what it is you think I should know."

Royden made a sound and turned away to walk a few paces before facing her again. "The best place for you is far from me. I should have Guy come and erase me from the memories of everyone here. You think I'm some…"—he waved his hands around, searching for a word—"I doona know what, but I'm not. I'm flawed. Extremely so."

"Everyone is."

His lips flattened. "I'm very aware of my shortcomings. I can pretend to fit in with humans, but I doona belong there."

"Let me tell you a little secret," she said. "None of us really fit in anywhere. We pretend until we find another person that makes us feel as if we fit in. If we're lucky, we find more than one, but some people don't even get that."

Royden stared at her for a long time before he shook his head. "Doona think I'm more than I am."

"I can't do that if I don't know what you are. I'm asking again. Tell me who you are. Tell me about your origins. Tell me the things you don't want me to know."

"You're asking a lot."

"I am," she replied with a smile. "And you're going to give it to me."

There was a barest hint of a smile. "Am I?"

"Yes."

"Why?"

"Because you want me to know."

He blew out a breath that ended in a chuckle. "Damn, if you are no' right."

That made her grin.

He scratched the back of his neck. "If you really want to know…"

"I think we've come to the conclusion I really want to know."

"This planet, this realm," he began. "It was once ruled by dragons. There were none of your kind here. From the dawn of this realm, it was dragons. All sizes, all colors. Each clan was ruled by a King, a Dragon King chosen by magic."

She blinked. "Chosen?"

"The magic looked into the hearts of every dragon. If there was one strong enough in strength and magic with purity in his heart, then they were chosen to be King. I was such a dragon."

Chills raced down Annita's back. She could certainly see Royden as a Dragon King.

"Some Kings took their place after the previous King had been killed in battle. Because only a Dragon King can kill a Dragon King. However, most of us have to challenge the current King and fight to the death to claim our positions."

She made a face. "But couldn't anyone claim to have the magic and tell them they were meant to be King?"

"Aye. But you know when the magic chooses you. It's a feeling you can no' dismiss. And if you are no' chosen by the magic and issue a challenge, then the current King would easily defeat you."

"Oh," she replied, brows raised.

Royden shrugged. "I never dreamed I'd be King to my clan. It was an honor I took seriously. I still take it seriously, even though my dragons are gone."

That took her aback. "Gone? How can they be gone?"

"It all started with the arrival of your kind."

Chapter Eight

He hadn't meant to tell her anything. In fact, Royden had decided it was better for Annita not to know any more about him, the Dragon Kings, or magic. He wasn't sure why he'd changed his mind. But with her standing there looking at him with such interest and determination, he hadn't been able to refuse her.

And if he were honest, it had a lot to do with the fact that she had wanted to see him in his true form.

A human had never asked that of him. Never one who was curious enough. Never one he'd allowed close enough to even know that side of him. Never one he couldn't seem to stay away from.

"Go on," she urged in a soft voice.

He hesitated, unsure now if he'd made the right decision. Annita was different from other mortals, but that didn't mean he should tell her everything. And it didn't go unnoticed by him that all the other Dragon Kings who had shared their past with females ended up mated to those same women.

Royden wasn't looking for a mate. He was happy as he was. With everything going on, having a mate—or even someone he was interested in—would only complicate things. And he'd been through that before. It might not have been a female, but his brother, which was just as bad.

"Royden? What is it?"

He ran a hand through his hair. "I'm no' sure I should go on."

"Why not? You can trust me."

"There have been few times in our history when a Dragon King could trust a mortal."

Her brow puckered. "I'm one you can trust. I've not told anyone your secrets. Any of them. I was meant to find you. Doesn't that tell you I can be trusted?"

"Nay, lass. It tells me you were meant to find a dragon."

She flattened her lips and shrugged. "I can't make you tell me. I wish there was something I could say so you would understand that I'm on your side."

Royden blew out a breath, watching her as she stared at him. "Why are you so interested?"

"You're a dragon," she said with a laugh. "I can't imagine anyone who wouldn't be interested."

"You've learned there are other beings on this realm with you. Beings who are no' only immortal but also have magic, and you are no' afraid?"

She gave him a flat look. "I'd be lying if I said it didn't give me pause. Everything we know as humans leads us to believe we're the only ones on this planet—realm," she corrected. "To learn about you is scary. But it's also exciting. We've always been told magic isn't real, that it's something made up by others. And yet, it is real. So are dragons. That in itself makes me smile."

"Even though those beings could wipe you out of existence?"

"Well," she said as she blew out a breath. "You could do that. But you haven't."

Royden chuckled and held out his hand to her. When she took it, he pulled her along with him against the far wall so they could sit. When they were comfortable, he continued. "Dragons communicate telepathically. There was no reason for us to speak using our voices. That changed the day a small group of mortals arrived here. Constantine, the King of Dragon Kings, called us all together. When we faced the humans, the magic of this realm gave us the ability to shift into your form so we could communicate. We were able to speak with the mortals. We discovered they had no magic and no way of protecting themselves. We made a pact then and there to give them shelter, aid, and to protect them. Some land was given to them, and we helped them build homes. We showed them how to fashion weapons and to hunt."

"They had no idea where they came from?" Annita asked with a frown.

He shook his head. "They knew their names, but nothing else. They didna know where they came from, how they got here, or why. It's one of the reasons we took pity on them."

"I'm surprised you did. Their arrival raises all sorts of red flags for me. Did none of you question it?"

"We all questioned it, but we could find nothing. And while you have nothing to compare to, I'll tell you that dragon magic is the strongest magic on this realm. At least, by itself."

"What does that mean?" she asked.

He waved away her words. "I'll get to that later. My point is, we were concerned and did all we could to figure out how the mortals came here. We could've killed them right then. Some might argue it would've been better if we had."

Annita moved a lock of wet hair that fell in her face. "But you didn't."

"Nay. For a time, everything was fine. The mortals were left to themselves, and the dragons continued on as they had. However, your kind produces children at a shocking rate. Soon, there wasna enough property. We gave up more land. And then more. And more."

"I can see where this is going," she said with a frown.

Royden looked at the water in the cave and noticed how the morning sun reflected on it. "We helped the humans fashion weapons to kill lesser animals for food. Because we helped them, we believed they would respect all dragons, no matter the size. There were smaller dragons. No larger than a cat. They were hunted. We went to the humans and managed to produce a truce where no dragons were to be destroyed. Ever."

"I gather that didn't last long."

"No' nearly long enough. Because clans were losing land, and our food was also being eaten by the mortals, some dragons became resentful. They lashed out. By eating humans."

Annita didn't so much as blink. "What did the people expect? Not that I condone the eating of my kind, but they went after the dragons first. Not to mention, they weren't respecting the fact that this wasn't their homeland."

"Your words surprise me," Royden confessed.

"I've always had a different view of things. It irritates my sister."

They shared a smile before he went back to the story. "Another meeting was called. This time, it took longer to work out the truce. I should add that by now, mortals were on dragon land all around the realm. There wasna a single clan that didna also have humans. Many Kings often interacted with the mortals and welcomed them into their homes. Some even took humans as lovers."

Annita's gaze raked over him. "I can understand why."

"The peace we once had between our two species was quickly dwindling with seemingly no way of reversing it. However, one of us, Ulrik, fell in love with a mortal. Dragons mate for life."

"Wait," she said and shifted positions. "If you're immortal and we're mortal, how does that work?"

Royden twisted his lips. "Well, as I mentioned, dragons mate for life. While we live for thousands of years, the magic ensures that a Dragon King can live much, much longer. And the magic makes sure that our mates do as well. Meaning, when a King and his mate go through the mating ceremony, the mate will live as long as the King does."

"So," Annita said, drawing out the word. "You're saying a mate to a Dragon King is essentially immortal as well."

"Aye. Only a Dragon King can kill another King. And a mate will only die when her King does."

Annita's eyes grew round. "Wow. Did this human marrying Ulrik know this?"

"Nay. Ulrik was going to surprise her with the news after they were mated."

"I'm not so sure that was a good idea."

Royden shrugged. "There are differing views on it to be sure, but it was a secret we kept from mortals so they wouldna try to find a King as a husband."

"I can absolutely see that. And what of children?"

"There has never been a child born to a Dragon King and a mortal. Most women miscarry after a few months. The rare who carried to term had bairns that were stillborn."

Annita winced. "Did the mortal know this?"

"It was common knowledge. Ulrik didna care that he would never have children. He was one of the best men I'd ever met. And he fell hard for the human. However, Con was his best friend, and Con had his doubts as to the mortal's true feelings for Ulrik. So, he followed her. Turns out, he had a right to be wary. She, along with a Druid and Ulrik's uncle, plotted to kill Ulrik."

"That was a lot of information right there. I'm dying to know about

Druids, but first, continue on with the other."

Royden glanced at the rocky ground beneath them. "Con knew that Ulrik would be devastated when he learned of this. Instead, Con called all of us together and sent Ulrik on a mission alone. While Ulrik was gone, we went after the mortal."

"By *go after*, I take it to mean you killed her."

"Aye."

Annita thought about that for a moment. "I can't say I agree with that, but I also wasn't there. I wasn't a part of everything that happened."

"We didna take it lightly. The truce between our races was on shaky ground, and Ulrik's marriage could've healed some of that. However, had the marriage taken place, and she tried to kill Ulrik on their wedding night as planned, she would've learned that he couldna die. Moreover, Ulrik would've gone berserk knowing the woman he'd chosen as his mate didna love him. He would've lost his mind. Who knows what would have happened?"

She wrinkled her nose. "That's a good point. So what did happen? Because something obviously did."

"While we hoped that taking care of Ulrik's problem wouldna result in war, we were wrong. When we told Ulrik, he was angry at us and the mortals, but in the back of his mind, he knew we'd tried to help. He didna come after us. He called his Silvers and went after the humans, beginning our war.

"The verra thing we'd tried to avoid happened anyway. However, Ulrik and his Silvers were no' the only ones attacking. After years of dealing with the ungrateful mortals, everyone but Con and his Golds began attacking. Even me."

Annita reached over and put her hand atop his. "You say that as if you're ashamed."

"I am. I killed those I swore to protect."

"You didn't do it because you liked it. You did it because you were betrayed. I'm not saying I agree with what any of you did—because I believe in life, not death. Although, I can admit to understanding why you joined the others."

Royden wrapped his fingers around hers, liking the way it felt to hold her. "Con is King of Kings because he's the strongest in both magic and power among all the Kings. He's in that position for a reason, and it showed then. He gradually drew us back to him, one by one. And when those of us who began protecting the mortals found that our dragons were being killed by them, we all knew we had crossed a line in the sand.

"Everyone but Ulrik obeyed Con and returned to Dreagan. Eventually, even many of the Silvers heeded Con until it was only Ulrik and his four largest Silvers going after the mortals. We all realized then that there were two options. Had Ulrik no' been so angry, he would've seen it, too. We could either wipe out the mortals once and for all and go back to the way things were. Or we could remember the vows we took and stop fighting."

Annita sighed softly and squeezed her eyes closed for a moment. "You stopped fighting."

"Aye. We were no' monsters. We realized that to keep true to ourselves, we needed to give up our realm. That meant sending the dragons away. We used our magic, and for the first time, created a dragon bridge to send them to another realm. We had no idea if they would be welcomed or even survive, but at least they had a better chance than they did here. Sending my family and clan away was the hardest thing I've ever done. It was then that my brother told me where he'd hidden the claw. I couldna return to find it as we still had Ulrik and his Silvers to take care of.

"I and the other Kings used our magic to trap the four Silvers and put them to sleep. We then took them to Dreagan and put them in a mountain where they remain to this day. Ulrik was another matter. He made it so Con didna have a choice but to strip him of his magic, forcing him to live as a human unable to shift into his true form. Then he banished Ulrik from Dreagan as we each went to our mountains to sleep while the mortals forgot about us."

Annita shook her head. "I don't know what to say. You gave up everything for us. We never would've done that. And banishing Ulrik? Why?"

"Because while we might have been hiding, Dreagan was ours, and no human could step on the land because of the magic surrounding it. Ulrik couldna use his magic or shift, and Con didna want to force him to bear witness to *us* shifting, which would have made things worse for Ulrik. Although, it wouldna have mattered what Con did. Ulrik's hatred turned to each of us. He spent eons as a human plotting our demise. He even went so far as to join forces with the Dark Fae in order to see it done."

Chapter Nine

"Dark Fae?" Annita repeated. "Based on that name alone, I suspect they aren't good people."

"They aren't people at all, at least as you know them," Royden told her. "They're Fae. They're from another realm, but a civil war destroyed it, and they came here."

She raised a brow. "You didn't make them leave after what happened with the humans? Or did they come before?"

"They came after the mortals. Let me back up and tell you about the Druids. Some humans who came here developed magic. They became Druids. Many were forced from their homes since mortals compared any magic to that of the dragons. The largest concentration of Druids still resides on the Isle of Skye in Scotland. Though, through the years, more Druids bore children with humans, who didna have power, diluting the magic and making Druids rarer and rarer. The Druids themselves split into two sects. The *mies*, or Druids who use their magic for good. And the *droughs*, those who aligned with the devil."

Annita released a breath. "I've heard of Druids. How is that possible, but I've not heard of dragons or Fae?"

"You've heard of the Fae. Fairies?"

"The Fae sound much different than fairies. The fairies I know of are small creatures with wings."

"But they have magic," Royden said. "While the Fae doona have wings, they do, for all intents and purposes, look verra much like mortals. They also have two sects. The Light Fae and the Dark Fae. The Light Fae have silver eyes and black hair. The Dark have red eyes and silver in their black hair."

Annita cocked her head to the side. "Why such different looks? Do the Druids look different?"

"You wouldna know if a Druid is a *mie* or a *drough* just by looking at them. The Dark Fae are different because the moment they kill their first person, their eyes turn red. The more evil they do, the more silver appears in their hair."

"That's good to know. I've never seen anyone like that here."

Royden shrugged. "There have no doubt been Fae here. They can use glamour to change their appearance so you wouldna know them. However, they're stunning. More beautiful than seems possible."

"I've known some people like that. You, for instance," she told him with a smile.

He chuckled, giving her a scorching look. "Thank you for the compliment, but I can assure you, I'm no' Fae. Now, mortals are inexplicably drawn to the Fae. They can no' control themselves."

Annita nearly told him that she was hard-pressed to control herself around *him*, but she kept that part to herself.

"The bad thing is, once a human has sex with a Light Fae, they can never be satisfied by another mortal again. Only a Fae can give them pleasure. The Light are thereby only allowed to have sex with a human once."

Annita raised a brow. "You'd think because of that, they wouldn't be allowed to have sex with us at all. Does it happen often?"

"Verra. There are many Halflings on this realm."

"And the Dark? Are they allowed to have sex with us?"

His expression tightened. "The Dark doona stop at just once. They will search out humans and draw them in. It's how they feed."

"I'm sorry. What?" Annita asked, taken aback.

"The Dark feed on mortal souls. While you experience pleasure unlike any you've ever known as they have sex with you over and over again, they're draining you of your soul all the while."

Annita thought about that for a moment and shuddered. "It actually sounds like a decent way to go if you have to die. But, personally, I think it's horrendous."

"I tend to agree. We've long fought the Dark."

"Is their magic stronger than yours?"

"Nay. When they first came here, we fought both them and the Light. Then the Light joined us, and we defeated the Dark. But the Fae had nowhere to go. Their realm had been destroyed. We agreed to allow them to stay, but they had to remain in Ireland. The Light took the top half of the isle, and the Dark the bottom. No matter how hard we've tried, humans flock to Ireland at an alarming rate. Since we can't control that, we at least try to keep the Dark on the isle as much as we can."

Annita shook her head in bewilderment. "There's so much going on around me I didn't know about. I never thought of myself as isolated out here, but that's exactly what I am."

"You're no' isolated. You're protected. You should cherish what you have. Besides, there are those living alongside Fae that doona know it. So doona put yourself down for not knowing. Only a small fraction of mortals know what I'm telling you."

She chuckled and looked at their joined hands. "That does make me feel a little better. So, all this time, you've been hiding?"

"No' the entire time. We eventually came out of hiding and walked among the mortals. Con realized that, in order for us to maintain our privacy and still be a part of this world, we needed to have a business. We began Dreagan Industries, our whisky company, and it has supported us. People visit the distillery every year, but they go no further than that. They think they know us, but no one really does."

"I can't blame you there. What about your dragons?"

His eyes lowered as he shrugged. His gaze then slid back to her. "We doona know. The Dark are no' our only enemies. We recently discovered a group called the Others. They're made up of *mies* and *droughs* from our realm, Dark and Light Fae, as well as *mies* and *droughs* from another realm. The verra realm where your kind originally came from. They joined their magic together, and we've come to find out it's enough to best ours."

It was a good thing Annita was sitting down because she was sure her legs would've given out on her. "Another realm?"

"You're from another realm. Everyone born there was born with magic. But the empress took advantage of her magic and used a spell that made her immortal. She aged, but verra, verra slowly. The more magic she took, the more babies were born without magic. She took those without magic and brought them here once she found our realm and the magic within it. She wants to rid this world of dragons so she can have it."

Annita tightened her fingers on Royden's. "That can't happen. I know I barely know you, but that can't happen. This is your home. You've already given up so much. Please tell me you're fighting."

"We're fighting," he said with a smile. "We're fighting with all we have."

"Good." The relief that spread through her was so strong, she became lightheaded.

"Do you regret knowing now?"

She shook her head. "Not at all. I wish I could help, but I don't regret any of it."

"And when I leave?"

Annita hoped her face remained impassive despite the immediate response of "*no*" that she shouted in her mind. She didn't want him to leave. Ever. But it was ridiculous to imagine that he'd remain. This might have been his home once, but now, it was in Scotland.

"How many of there are you?" she asked instead.

"At Dreagan? Many."

While he had told her much, she wasn't at all upset that he wouldn't tell her an exact number. With the Others, it made sense to keep some things a secret. "How long will you stay in Greece?"

"I doona know. I should return soon."

"Then we must make the most of our time together," she said as she got to her feet and pulled him up with her.

He grinned, his blue eyes crinkling at the corners. "What do you have in mind?"

"A swim."

Royden glanced away as he gave a nod. "I agree. There's something I want to show you."

"I know every inch of these caves. There isn't anything you could show me that I don't already know."

"Is that a challenge?" he asked with a smile.

She found herself grinning. "It is."

"Challenge accepted. Ready?"

Annita gave a nod. "Absolutely."

He released her hand and dove into the water. Right before his body went under, his clothes vanished, replaced by swim trunks. She gasped when she saw the tattoo that took up his entire back. She wasn't given time to see much of it, however. Annita then followed him into the water and came up for air beside him.

"What?" he asked.

She wanted to look at his tattoo, but she couldn't see it well in the water. She'd just have to wait until they were on land again. Annita shook her head. "Nothing."

"I take it you're a strong swimmer."

"I am."

"You're going to need to be. If you get in trouble, let me know."

"I should be fine."

He flashed her a wide grin. "Then follow me."

When he swam out of the cave, she was right beside him. Annita kept pace with him easily. She followed him around boulders, moving in behind him to keep out of currents and away from the larger rocks that could cause damage. She swam every day. Long distances, too. But she found that she began to tire. When she paused to look around, she realized that they had swum far from the cave.

She turned and began swimming again now that she had lagged behind him. Her arms were tiring quickly. Then they finally stopped.

"Do you trust me?"

She treaded water and said, "I do."

"I willna let anything happen to you. You need to take a deep breath. You willna be able to swim fast enough. I'll have to take you."

"Fast enough for what?"

His eyes held hers. "To see something no one else has seen since my clan last inhabited this isle."

That was an opportunity she wasn't going to pass up. She began taking deep breaths. Then she gave him a nod and sucked in a large lungful. Royden grabbed her hand and pulled her below water. He then wrapped an arm around her, bringing her against him. Annita was shocked at how fast they moved.

Then again, he was a dragon.

The deeper they went, the more pressure pushed against her. She popped her ears and released some air when her lungs began to burn. She tried to see where he was taking her, but she couldn't see anything other than what was usually below the water.

She squeezed her eyes closed when her lungs throbbed, and she released more air. There wasn't much left for her to use. She had to pop her ears twice more. She clung to Royden, hoping they returned to the surface soon. Instead, he swam faster.

Annita was now out of air. She really wanted to see whatever it was that Royden wanted to show her, but she couldn't. She needed oxygen. She tapped his shoulder to get his attention. They were moving so fast, things were a blur. She spotted something moving out of the corner of her eye and turned her head to see a huge boulder roll out of the way, seemingly on its own. Annita knew Royden was responsible.

They went even deeper to the opening the rock had covered. Annita struggled against him. She needed air. But he held her tighter. After they went through the entrance, he gave her a hard shove upward. Annita didn't know where she was going or what was happening. She couldn't even control anything since she was propelled upward.

Just when she thought her lungs might burst, her head suddenly broke the water's surface, and she sucked in a huge mouthful of air. She treaded water and closed her eyes as oxygen filled her body. She then opened her eyes and was met with blackness.

There was a sound beside her that she sincerely hoped was Royden. A moment later, a ball of light rose above her and shed its rays all over, brightening the cavern. She gaped at how high the light continued to rise, as if there were no ceiling above them.

"Are you all right?" Royden asked.

She jerked her head to him. "Where are we?"

He smiled and motioned with his head. "Follow me."

Though her body was tired, she swam after him until they reached the edge. He jumped out easily and helped her up. He then linked his fingers with hers and tugged her along after him as they began walking.

The light looked as though it had finally stopped rising. It was a speck above them but shone like the sun. Royden held out his hand, and another ball of light appeared, racing ahead of them to a tunnel that was large enough to fit a dragon.

There were no words spoken as they meandered through the maze of tunnels. They were dry, proving that no water filled them. The rock was worn smooth, however. There was nothing that hurt the bottom of her bare feet. It was a little chilly, but she didn't mind it because she was so fascinated with everything around her.

Finally, Royden stopped. The light with them flew upwards like a rocket to shine like the other. If she'd thought the cavern they'd swum into was big, this one was three times its size. It looked as if there were raised sections almost like seats in a semicircle. As she turned, she found one lone perch sitting before the rest.

"My seat," Royden said in a solemn voice.

He released her hand and walked to it. As a human, he had to put his hands on the stone and jump to stand on it. Then he turned and faced her. But he didn't look at her. His gaze was on the seating area, and she knew he was thinking about the time when this had been his home.

Chapter Ten

He was home. Royden hadn't intended to come here. It would dredge up memories, and he was better off without them. Then he'd told Annita of his past. The next thing he knew, he'd wanted to show her this.

It was folly. He'd known that as he swam here. He could've turned back at any time, but he didn't. He kept swimming. Now that he was here, he was glad that he'd come. Some of the Kings had been able to return to where they once ruled. Just as he expected, there was a slew of bad memories, but there were good ones, as well.

"Shift," Annita urged him.

His gaze jerked to her. "What?"

"Change into your true form."

Royden hesitated for just a moment before he did as she asked. The last time he had stood in this spot, he had been talking to his clan. So much fear and anxiety had filled the cavern that day that it still remained. Emotion clogged his throat as he fought the wave of fury and regret that washed over him.

He felt something touch him and looked down to see Annita before him, her hand on his talon. Tears rolled down her face. Tears he couldn't—and wouldn't—shed. But she did it for him. She seemed to understand *everything*. He could barely fathom it, but there was no denying it.

"I'm glad you brought me here," she told him.

Royden lifted his head and looked at the emptiness before him, where the great Beige dragons had once stood. In order to face each day, the Dragon Kings had learned how to close off memories of the past and do their best not to think about their family or clans. Otherwise, everything they had done to survive would've crumbled.

But now, standing in his throne room, Royden's chest was heavy, filled with an ache of loneliness and wretchedness that would never be assuaged until his clan returned to the realm. Given that possibility was slim only made things worse.

It reminded him of how he'd felt when he took to his mountain on Dreagan. He had bellowed his fury at what had happened to their world. He'd scored the walls with his claws since he couldn't attack the mortals. He'd burned half the mountain with dragon fire and busted more rock.

The mountain shook time and again, but it never collapsed. It held steady. Eventually, his anger ran out. He sought out dragon sleep so he could forget everything. And he would've stayed that way had Con not woken those of them who hadn't wanted to be disturbed. Now, here he was, back in his old domain with a mortal who had been prophesied to find him.

He had no doubt in his mind that it was he that she had been meant to find. Royden still wasn't sure what it meant, but he was going to find out. Right now, however, he would remember his family and clan. It wasn't easy, though. He'd gone to such extremes not to think of the past.

The image of his brother was fading. The memories were still there, but he couldn't recall details of his brother as he used to. Time had done that. Some might call it easing his burden, but he felt as if he were losing the last thread to his family. He didn't want to lose it. Because if he did, he wasn't sure what he would have left.

At least both of his parents hadn't been alive to see what his reign as King of Beiges had come to. Not that he was to blame for everything that had happened. He realized that, but he still shouldered some of the blame. He, like the other Kings, had agreed to shelter the mortals when they arrived.

They had come so close to wiping out the humans when Ulrik attacked them. Would it have been better for them had that happened? For a long time, that was up for debate. However, with the arrival of the Others and all they had done to the Kings, Royden could now answer that.

His eyes lowered to Annita, who stood beside him, her hand still on him as she looked around the cavern. If they had annihilated the mortals, she wouldn't be here. He wouldn't have learned her smile, her sharp mind, or her kindness. He wouldn't have beheld her stunning body or the way her eyes seemed to see straight through to his soul. He wouldn't know her.

And that would be a shame.

Yet his family would be here. None of the dragons would've had to leave. Ulrik wouldn't have been banished, the Fae would've been driven out, and they wouldn't have the Others to contend with. V wouldn't have had his memories altered, and none of them would've spent eons deep in dragon sleep as the centuries passed.

Before he'd met Annita, Royden would've said that's exactly what should've happened. Hell, if he had the ability, he would've gone back in time to change things.

But what would the killing of the mortals have done to the Kings? How many of them would've actually remained Kings after the war? None of them would be alive today, of that Royden was certain. And none of the Kings who had found their mates among humans would be happy right now.

The decisions of the past were no longer so cut and dried. Perhaps they had never been. But he was only seeing that now. There were a good many Kings who had found love and happiness with mortals, and even Fae. How could that be wrong?

Yet, in order to have that, the Kings had had to lose everything. That's what didn't make sense to him. It might never, simply because he wasn't meant to know such things. He could go around and around about this in his mind to try and figure out what they should have done. The simple truth, however, was that everything happened for a reason.

He didn't want to admit that, but there was no way to refute it. Everyone had a path. Some called it destiny, others Fate. The decisions a person made on that path affected everything after in a ripple effect. He could look back and say a certain decision was the wrong one, but if he looked down the line and saw the good—and possibly great—things that had occurred because of that wrong decision, was it then really wrong?

Perhaps he'd come to this same conclusion long ago in dragon sleep, which allowed him to co-exist with the mortals so easily. Whatever the reason, Royden knew that he was supposed to meet Annita. Just as she was supposed to meet him. Fate or destiny, it didn't matter. It was what it was.

Now, as he looked out over the cavern, the weight of the past didn't rest so heavily on him. He didn't think about his brother or clan because not knowing if they survived or where they were would likely drive him insane. All he could do was hope that they were safe and happy. Because none of the dragons knew what had happened to the Kings, either.

No matter what, this was Royden's life now. And he was going to fight for it. Not just because some group was coming after the Kings, but because this was his home, and that of the mortals he and the other Kings had sworn to protect. That wasn't going to stop now.

Royden shifted to his mortal form. Annita's head swiveled to him, and she gave him a gentle smile when he dropped down beside her. He linked their hands together and looked about the cavern. "I was the last to leave this place. I put the boulder over the entrance to make sure it would stay hidden."

"I would've done the same. I'm honored that you brought me here."

He smiled and glanced at her. "I didna mean it to be so depressing."

"This was your life. Of course you were going to be bombarded with emotions. How could you not?"

Royden swallowed, shrugging. "I wasna thinking about that when I decided to bring you. I wanted to show you something that no other mortal had seen before."

She turned to face him, her eyes shining brightly. "It's beautiful. And you, standing on your throne, looking out over all of this is utterly magnificent."

"I wish you could've seen all the dragons."

"I do. In here," she said, tapping her temple.

He smoothed back a lock of hair from her face. "You are truly unique, do you know that?"

"I'm nothing special."

"I disagree wholeheartedly. Everything about you from the first moment we met has been the exact opposite of what I thought. I may have remained in Crete to find out more about the prophecy, but you are the one who occupies my thoughts."

Her gaze briefly lowered. "Do I?"

"Does that surprise you?"

"It does. A man like you must have thousands of lovers."

He shook his head and moved closer to her. "There is no one who holds my heart."

"Because you won't give it away?"

"I thought that was the case, but I've recently discovered that it's because I've no' found the right someone to claim it."

Her brown eyes blinked up at him solemnly. "I know exactly what you mean."

"Then you know how good it feels to finally meet someone who might be able to do just that."

"I do," she said and moved closer so their bodies brushed together.

Royden gently skimmed the pads of his fingers down her face before he slid his hand around to the back of her neck. "I've dreamed of kissing your lips."

The pulse at her throat beat erratically as she gazed up at him. "And I've dreamed of you kissing me."

His head lowered, and their lips met. Heat infused him—a hunger for Annita unlike anything he'd ever experienced before. He yearned to spin her around and lay her back on the slab of rock so he could remove her clothes, but her kisses were so sensual, so inviting that he couldn't stop.

He deepened the kiss and wrapped his arms around her. She moaned and pressed her breasts against him, causing him to groan. His cock ached from needing to be inside her. Then Annita's hands began roaming over his body. The feel of her palms against his flesh only fanned the flames of his desire.

The tighter he held her, the deeper he kissed her, the more she responded. And the more he craved her.

Suddenly, she pulled away from him, ending the kiss. He reluctantly released her. The look on her face was filled with desire as she reached up and pulled the tie to her bikini top. In the next breath, it was on the floor.

Royden stared at her hardened nipples, his hands itching to cup the round globes. But his eyes were drawn to her fingers that hooked into the bottom of her bathing suit as she pushed it down over her hips and kicked it away.

His gaze raked over her from her beautiful breasts, to the indent of her waist, to the flare of her hips, her long, lean legs, and then back up to her smooth sex, devoid of any hair.

"Lass, you're so gorgeous, I can barely find the words."

Annita smiled and walked to him, but she didn't put her arms around him. Instead, she tugged down his swimming trunks.

Chapter Eleven

Never had she felt such desire before. Annita's body hummed with it. She licked her lips, tasting Royden's kiss as she did. She put her hands flat on his chest and caressed over his broad shoulders to his thick arms and back to his chest again. Her gaze briefly met his before she let her hands trail down his washboard stomach to his trim hips.

His cock strained between them, hard and waiting. She wrapped her hand around him, feeling his warmth. He was like silk over steel, so hard and yet smooth. She knelt before him, letting her other hand trail down his chest.

She raised her eyes and held his as she parted her lips and took him into her mouth. One of his hands tangled in her hair, holding her as his head dropped back, and his eyes closed. She drew him deep, using her hands, tongue, and lips up and down his shaft. His moans drove her onward, wanting to give him pleasure.

He pulled back and tugged her to her feet. "If you keep doing that, you'll finish me, and there's so verra much I want to do to you before that."

"What are you waiting for?"

His blue eyes darkened with desire before he kissed her. It was a kiss meant to show her how much he wanted her. It was a kiss that rocked her to her very bones. It was a kiss to curl her toes.

It accomplished all of that and more.

When he pulled away, she made a sound of protest. He chuckled and took her hand and led her from the room back into the tunnel. Her body throbbed with need. Thankfully, the light was with them once again. She tried to look at his back and the tattoo, but he kept her even with him.

It was like she was walking in a dream. She was in a strange place, and yet it was Crete. She was on land, and yet below water. She was with a man, yet a Dragon King. Annita looked at him and smiled.

She had no idea where he was taking her, and she didn't care so long as he was touching and kissing her. Finally, he turned, and she found herself walking downward. In the next heartbeat, she felt the steam from a thermal hot spring. Royden stopped and looked at her before he stepped backwards into the water. Annita followed him, sighing at the sensation of the warmth surrounding her.

"You were chilled," he said as he pulled her against him.

She shrugged. "I didn't feel it."

"I wouldna want you getting cold."

"I don't think that's possible with you beside me."

He turned her so that her back was to his chest. Her feet didn't touch the bottom, so she let him hold her. He then took her hands and stretched her arms out before bending them behind her. Her fingers brushed damp rock.

"Hold on to them," he whispered.

She did as he instructed. His hands then traveled down her arms to her shoulders and then cupped her breasts. Annita sucked in a breath at the exquisite pleasure that rushed through her when he rolled her nipples between his fingers.

Her eyes closed as the water lapped at her skin. Every nerve ending was ablaze with pleasure, with need that only one man, one *dragon* could quench—Royden.

One of his hands traveled down her stomach. She parted her legs, eager for him to touch her. He parted the folds of her sex before twirling a fingertip around her aching clit. With pleasure coming from both her sex and breasts, Annita found herself hurtling toward climax. Was it something in the water that pushed her so quickly? Was it the cave? Was it Royden?

She didn't know or care. Her eyes closed as she leaned her head back against him. His breath fanned her shoulder. Both of them were breathing heavily. At her back, she could feel his arousal pressing against her. Each time she moaned, his cock twitched.

"I've never seen anything so beautiful," Royden whispered.

She turned her face toward his. "I'm all yours."

"Doona tell a King that. Doona tell me that."

Annita opened her eyes to look at him. "But it's the truth."

"It's the pleasure talking."

At that moment, he gave her nipple a light pinch. She gasped at the pleasure as her sex throbbed. In response, he slipped a finger inside her. In and out, his digit moved in a slow, steady rhythm.

"No," she said when she found her voice. "It's you."

Royden's lips wrapped around her earlobe and suckled. His hand continued its assault on her sex while his thumb circled her swollen clit as he teased her nipple. She was bombarded on all sides by pleasure drawing her closer and closer to orgasm. Desire tightened low in her belly as she began the fascinating, thrilling spiral to ecstasy.

She was on the precipice, ready to fall into the waiting arms of pleasure when Royden's hands were suddenly gone. Dazed, she opened her eyes to discover he'd turned her so they were facing each other. If she thought she would finally have him inside her, she was mistaken.

He put her hands on the stone once more just as before. Then he grabbed her hips and lifted them until she was floating on her back. Annita watched him, her heart rate kicking up a notch when he spread her legs and settled between them. She moaned his name when he licked her sex, stopping at her clit.

Just like that, she was right back into pleasure. She closed her eyes, dropping her head into the water. This time, she knew he would allow her to peak. She was already so close. It wouldn't take much. Or so she thought.

His tongue licked, laved at his leisure. As if he didn't have anything else to do but feast upon her. Every time her body tightened as she got close to orgasm, he would change up what he was doing and make her go through it all again.

No one had ever paid her so much attention before. No one had ever cared about what she felt. No one had wanted to give her so much pleasure before. And she knew in that instant that no one but Royden ever would. Her thoughts didn't stay there long as her eyes flew open, her mouth parted in an O when he pushed two fingers inside her. He pumped them within her while he continued flicking his tongue over her clit.

She tried to keep still, to keep her body relaxed when the orgasm built. But her body took over. Except this time, Royden didn't stop. A white-hot light exploded behind her eyelids as she climaxed.

* * * *

Royden fought to keep control of himself at the feel of Annita's body tightening around his fingers as she peaked. The sight of her flushed skin, her mouth parted in a silent scream made him want her even more.

He wanted to give her several more orgasms before he filled her, but he couldn't hold off anymore. With her body still convulsing, he pulled her against him and entered her. Her arms came around him instantly. They looked into each other's eyes, and something happened. Royden couldn't pinpoint what it was. It could've been the cosmos shifting or a star being born, but he knew that they might have entered this private world as two separate people, but they would be leaving as one.

Her fingers threaded in his hair. "Don't stop. Don't ever stop."

He didn't need to be told twice. Royden pulled out of her until only the head of his shaft remained, then he thrust into her once more. Again and again he repeated the movements, his tempo increasing.

They never stopped looking at each other. Invisible bonds wove through them, around them, binding them to each other. It was too late to stop it now, and he didn't want to. Fate had set each of them on this course. He couldn't hold back if he wanted to.

He moved them to the side of the pool. With one hand on her back to keep her from scraping against the rocks, he grabbed the boulder with his other hand and began thrusting fast and deep. Her legs wrapped around his waist as she moved against him. The water churned, their breaths mixed, and the passion grew higher and higher.

The moment he felt her nails dig into him, Royden knew she was close to another orgasm. He gave her a nod, telling her to let go. When she did, when he felt her body clamping tightly around his cock, he let his climax take him.

He didn't know how long they stayed locked together after their bodies had finally stopped moving. Annita's head rested on his shoulder. He drew in a breath and moved away from the side so he could hold her with both arms. Neither said a word. Steam rose up as if shrouding them from the world. In many ways, it did just that.

Here, in this place, the rest of the world didn't exist. It was just the two of them.

Annita turned her head and placed a kiss on his neck. He smiled, amazed at how content he felt. His body was pleasured, but his soul was…happy. Happy like he had never been before. And he knew the mortal he held in his arms was the reason.

"I used to tell myself I didna want a mate," he said. "I gave all kinds of reasons that seemed more than valid at the time."

She lifted her head to look at him and wiped beads of sweat from his brow. "And now?"

"Now, there's only one thing I want."

"What's that?"

"You." He swallowed and shook his head. "You've taken my heart, and you didna even know. I didna know it until a few moments ago."

A slow smile spread over Annita's face.

He wanted to return it, but he couldn't. "We barely know each other, and you have a life here. In the short time we've been together, the pain I've carried since the day the dragons left is gone. You've stopped that."

"Then why are you frowning?"

"Because I want you. I crave you like air in my lungs. I know you're my mate, but I know the kind of world I live in. There's no guarantee we'll best the Others. I doona want to pull you into my world only to see you hurt."

Annita cupped her hand to his face. "Tell me this. If the Others do happen to succeed, what happens to the humans here in this realm?"

He was silent, unable to tell her how bad it could be.

"That's what I figured," she said. "If I have the opportunity to be with you, then I want it. I don't care how short or how long the time. I want to be with you."

"You say that without knowing how bad things can be for the Kings."

"I say that knowing how good it feels to be with you. My mother used to tell me that I'd know when I found the right person. That I'd feel it here," she said and touched her chest. "I knew the moment I saw you. The more time I spend with you, the more sure I am. I know you've lived thousands of years, and you've probably loved several times—"

He gave a shake of his head. "Nay. I've no'."

"You told me earlier that dragons mate for life. You just told me I was your mate. That means you know, just like I do. And don't you dare think it's because I care about your wealth or the fact that I'll become immortal. Royden, I only want you. You bring such joy to my life, and you make my heart sing."

He pulled her against him for a hug and closed his eyes. His halfhearted attempt to change her mind about him had failed, and he was glad for it. But a part of him still worried about her. He would always worry, whether she was with him or not. Because she was his mate.

Chapter Twelve

Annita hadn't wanted to leave the cave, but they both knew she had to get back before people came looking for her. When they broke the surface, the sun was making its descent into the horizon.

"Come back with me," she urged him.

Royden hesitated as they treaded water. "They'll wonder how I got here."

"I'll tell them I invited you."

He grinned. "Let's head back, then. You need some food."

"I'm hungry. Not sure it's for food."

That made him laugh. She was grinning as she began swimming. When they reached the beach, they walked from the water, holding hands. So much in her life had been confusing, but that wasn't the case with Royden. Everything was now clear and obvious. Almost as if she had been in a dream world before him. His arrival had shaken up everything in her life, and she was glad for it.

She dried off and looked up at the house.

"You've never lived anywhere else," Royden said.

Annita turned to him and shrugged. "So? A lot of people can say that."

"If you need time, I understand. I can leave and return in a few months."

"Why would you do that?" she asked with a frown. "I want only you. Will I miss my family? Of course. But I can see them."

Royden looked away without saying anything.

She stared at him for a moment, trying to figure out what he wasn't telling her. Then it struck her. He was immortal. The other Dragon Kings were immortal. They couldn't continue to be around people decade after decade without others noticing that they didn't age. And her family would notice.

"Oh," she said.

His gaze slid to her. "It's a lot to ask. No' only will you no' be able to see your family after a while, but there willna be children."

Annita had forgotten that part. She'd always thought to have kids of her own one day. Just as she expected to marry and live on the family estate. She would have to give all of that up if she went with Royden. She loved her family dearly. Could she live without them? Could she turn away from everything she knew to something entirely different?

As she stared at Royden, she thought about how she felt with him. How he made her smile, how he made her laugh with the things he said, how his kisses made her sigh, and how his touch brought her ecstasy. With him, she would have a love she had been waiting for. With him, she would have adventure and magic. With him, she would have a kind of life they wrote about in fairy tales.

Annita walked around him to look at his back. Twice now, she had caught a glimpse of his tattoo, but she hadn't really gotten to look at it. She took the opportunity because she didn't know what to say to him.

The moment her eyes found the ink, she was awestruck. She had seen some good work before, but this was beyond anything she could describe. It wasn't black but a combination of black and red, making the design something altogether different.

The dragon spread across the entirety of his back. It looked as if the beast were flying, his wings spread out, and his head staring directly at her. It was a straightforward design that was anything but simple. The attention to detail on every scale was mesmerizing—just as the dragon's eyes were. It took her a moment because she was so enamored with the tat, but she realized that this dragon was a replica of Royden, right down to his eyes.

She put her hand on the dragon and felt the heat of Royden's body. Annita closed her eyes, and for just an instant, she could've sworn she felt something move beneath her palm. Her eyes snapped open, but she didn't remove her hand.

Royden's head shifted to the side to look at her over his shoulder. "When the mortals arrived and we shifted, a tattoo appeared on each of us. We also have swords."

She met his gaze and swallowed as she dropped her hand. Royden turned to face her. She wanted to go with him, but something held her back, yet she couldn't figure out what it was. All her life, she'd known that she was destined to find a dragon. But never in her wildest dreams had she believed that dragon would also be a man that she felt herself falling for. Never did she think she could have a future with him.

"It's all right," Royden told her. "I understand that being with me means you'll give up a family you're close to."

She licked her lips. "I never thought I'd have to give up my family to be with the man I chose to give my heart to."

He took her hand and brought it to his lips. "Take some time. All of this has happened quickly. Think over everything. I'll return in a week. If you've chosen to be with me, then meet me in the cave at noon. If you have no', then I'll have your answer."

When his hand loosened on hers, she tightened her fingers, not wanting to release him. "Don't go."

"It willna do you any good if I remain."

"I disagree."

His smile was sad as he pulled her against him and gave her a long, languid kiss. When he finally ended it, he looked down at her and moved some hair from her face. "I'll return in a week."

This time when she tried to hold him, he pulled her hands away and kissed them. Annita remained in the shallow water as the waves rolled against her while Royden walked deeper into the sea and then dove beneath the surface. And just like that, he was gone.

Annita felt bereft. She wanted to call him, to tell him that she'd made her decision, but…she couldn't. A tear fell down her face, and she hastily wiped it away. How could this have been the best day of her life and yet have ended so horribly? Royden was who she wanted. She didn't care that he was immortal or a dragon. She wanted *him*.

His smile, his touch, his lips against hers.

She had no idea how long she stood there before the sound of a seagull startled her. Annita jumped and turned to see if anyone was around. When she realized that she was still alone, she went to her towel and wrapped it around her. Then she began the journey up to the house. She managed to get inside and to her room without encountering anyone. The second she heard voices, she diverted her route because she wasn't in the mood to talk.

Once in her room, she took a long shower, letting the hot water slide over her. It reminded her of the hot spring and the way Royden had made love to her. He'd brought her to heights she hadn't known were possible. The way he'd looked at her with such longing and hunger made her stomach feel as if hundreds of butterflies were inside her.

Her skin began to wrinkle when she shut off the water and got out. She wrapped her hair in a towel and put on her robe to stand before her closet. But it wasn't clothes she saw. It was Royden. Everywhere she looked, she saw him.

Annita walked to her bed and lay down to look at the ceiling. She knew it was time for dinner, but she wouldn't be able to eat, and her family would notice, which meant they'd ask questions. She couldn't handle any of that tonight. She was reaching for her phone to send a text like a coward when there was a knock on her door.

"Yes?" she called out.

The door opened, and her mother walked in, concern in her brown eyes. "Everything all right?"

"I'm okay."

"You don't look it."

Her mother had always had an innate ability to know when something was wrong. Annita shrugged and pulled the towel from her head. She went to drop it on the floor, but her mother took it and hung it up in the bathroom.

"I just need to be alone," Annita said.

Selini nodded as she walked back into the bedroom. "There's nothing wrong with that. If you need anything, we're here for you. Take all the time you need."

"Thanks, Mom."

She smiled and walked to the door and opened it. Then Selini paused and looked back at Annita. "Just thought I'd let you know that we all like Royden."

"That was out of the blue."

Her mother snorted loudly and very unladylike. "We have eyes, and we all saw the way the two of you looked at each other. That's special. It isn't something you should give up. Ever. It's something you fight for with all you have."

"He's not from here."

"So?" her mother asked with a shrug. "Maybe the man you choose lives here and we get to see you all the time. Maybe he lives in another country and we see you less often. It doesn't mean we stop being family. Do you love him?"

Annita glanced at the ceiling. "People don't fall for each other so quickly."

"Oh, yes they do. Your father and I did. You know when you know."

Her gaze lowered to her mother. "Would you have given up everything for Dad?"

"Yes. Is that what this is about? You giving up things here? You wouldn't be giving up anything."

Annita forced the best smile she could and shook her head. "I know that."

"Do you?" her mother asked with a raised brow. "You certainly don't sound like it. Tell me," she said as she shut the door and walked to the bed to sit on the end of it. "Have you thought about what life with Royden would be like as his wife?"

"Yes."

"And?"

Annita thought about that for a moment and shrugged. "It won't be easy."

"Nothing worth having is ever easy. His life is very different than ours, and no doubt it'll be an adjustment. For both of you. That's what happens with any marriage. Why don't you tell me what the real problem is?"

Annita parted her lips, ready to tell a lie. Instead, she told the truth. "If I choose Royden, I would rarely get to see you."

"We wouldn't make you come here all the time. Of course, we'd travel to see you, as well. And there's this new invention called a phone. One that can even be carried around with me all the time called a mobile phone."

Annita rolled her eyes and chuckled at her mother's sarcasm. "In other words, we could talk all the time."

"Exactly."

"There's something else."

"We figured out one problem. What's the other?"

She drew in a deep breath and sat up. "He can't have children."

"Oh," her mother said after a brief pause. "I know how much you've wanted to have your own. You could always adopt or foster children. There are ways around it."

Annita shook her head. "I'm not sure there are."

Selini's keen eyes blinked as she comprehended that there were things Annita hadn't told her. "I see. I can't help with this part. You'll have to come to terms with not being a mother."

"Is it all I think it is?" Annita asked.

"Yes. And no," her mother said with a smile. "I didn't necessarily want children. Chara told me I'd have them, so I accepted that. You and your sister have brought us incredible joy. We're beyond proud to have each of you in our lives. I wouldn't change any of it. But had Chara told me that I wouldn't have children, but would still have a long, happy life with your father, I would've taken that as well. Love defines a couple's life, not children. I've seen marriages I believed would last forever because of shared love crumble when there were no children. Don't let that be you. Children, if you have them, are a blessing. A joy. But whether you have them or not shouldn't determine if your love for the man you've chosen wanes or not."

Annita took her mom's hand and smiled. "Thank you. I needed to hear that."

Chapter Thirteen

The week was the slowest of Royden's life. He tried to leave Crete, but in the end, he decided to remain. He kept away from Annita and the estate, but he walked for hours at a time. He also drove all around the island, stopping at different beaches and simply looking out at the water, remembering a different time.

He had one more day until he was to swim to the cave and await Annita. Royden wasn't sure if she would come or not. He'd never been so nervous in his life. The drive around the island did little to pass the time. In fact, it only made things worse as he went out of his way not to travel past her home. Royden searched every face for hers, both grateful that he didn't find her and angry that he couldn't see her.

When he arrived back at the hotel, he parked the Vespa and headed inside. He paid attention to no one as he got into the elevator. It was only as the lift began its climb that he realized he wasn't alone.

"I was beginning to wonder if you'd notice me."

He turned his head and found himself looking into the face of Emilios. "My apologies. I was deep in thought."

"You and Annita both. As a father, I like to help my children out with their problems, or at least point them in the right direction. Unfortunately, I'm in a unique situation where I can't do anything. At least, with Annita. My beautiful wife filled me in on a few things."

There was a ding as they reached Royden's floor. He motioned with his hand for Emilios to step out, and then he followed him. They were silent as they walked to Royden's room. Inside, Royden watched as the patriarch of the Dragoumis family moved to the windows overlooking the sea.

"In all my years of marriage, I've told Selini everything. Everything, that is," he said and turned to Royden, "except about the conversation that Chara and I had regarding Annita and the prophecy."

Royden pushed away from the door and walked toward Emilios. "Why did you keep it from her?"

"Chara told me that I had to. I didn't ask why. It wouldn't have done any good. Sometimes, my aunt knew the reasons. But many times, she didn't. We learned to trust what she said."

"And what was it Chara told you?"

Emilios scratched his forehead and put his hands in his pants' pockets. "She warned me that Annita should only learn a portion of the prophecy. She alerted me that Annita had overheard her telling me and Selini of her prediction. Chara said that my mother should be the one to talk to Annita about it. I had no issue with that. Then she told me the rest of what she saw." He cleared his throat. "I know what you are, Royden. I didn't at first, but I figured it out after I saw you and Annita disappear together the night you came for dinner. I learned hours later that she had taken you to one of the storage rooms and showed you the picture of what was found on our land."

"Annita told you?" Royden asked.

Emilios shook his head. "There is very little that goes on in my home that I'm not privy to. There are eyes everywhere, and those who work for me are extremely loyal."

"So, they spied on us."

"Not how you may think. I asked if any of them had seen where you and Annita had disappeared to. That's why and when they told me. It wasn't as if they came running with the information."

Royden stared at Emilios, waiting for him to continue.

"I've had a long time to come to terms with what my aunt foretold. I wasn't sure how to react at first. Then she told me that the very thing that had saved our family would be what brought you to us. She said that while most believed it was a bone from a dinosaur, she knew it was a talon from the dragons who used to call our island home."

Royden hadn't been prepared for that.

Emilios continued. "Chara told me that you would come to us as a man, but you were really a dragon. You were the one Annita would find, and you would be the one to change her life forever. It meant that she would leave us and begin a new life with you, but it was her destiny as a mate to a Dragon King."

"Chara knew that as well?"

Emilios smiled, nodding. "My aunt's power was amazing."

"Why did she no' want Annita to know all of this?"

"She said that the decision rested with Annita. Chara might not have named you, but she said you would choose my daughter as your mate."

Royden glanced away. "Annita is making that decision now."

"I know. I've debated whether to come to you or not. My telling you won't change anything with my daughter, but I wanted you to know that we aren't trying to make Annita choose us. She has always had a mind of her own. More than that, I won't stand in the way of Chara's prophecy."

"Thank you."

But Emilios wasn't finished. "There's one more thing you should know. This was the most important of all the information Chara told me. She said that if Annita chooses you, then she'll be another spoke in an ever-growing wheel, strengthening all of you in your upcoming battle."

Royden felt as if he'd been kicked. "And if Annita doesna choose me?"

"I don't know. Chara didn't say anything about that."

"I remained on Crete because of the prophecy," Royden admitted. "Annita told me about it the first time we met, which was the day before I sought you out."

Emilios chuckled, his lips twisting. "She has always been one who runs headlong into any adventure. She's had a fascination with those caves since she learned how to swim. We used to try to keep her out of them, or at least go with her. It was Chara who told us that Annita needed to learn them. If Chara knew that Annita would find you in the caves, she didn't share that with me."

"I'm sad I didna get a chance to meet your aunt. I would've liked to talk to her."

"Funny you say that. Right before she died, she grabbed my hand and said, 'Tell him I would've welcomed him.' I didn't need to ask to know she was referring to you."

Royden smiled, truly touched by the words. "I love your daughter. Chara was right, Annita is my mate. I know Annita loves me, but the life we'll have is different than what she knows. You willna get to see her much."

"I'll still get to talk to my daughter, even if I don't get to see her. I want her happy, Royden. If that means with you in Scotland, living as a mate to a Dragon King, then I accept that. I know you'll protect her."

"You doona seem worried about the war your aunt spoke of."

Emilios gave him a flat look. "I'm more than worried about that. For all Chara's knowledge of you, she knew very little about the Dragon Kings. There is nothing out there about your kind, and I suspect it's because you've seen to that."

"We have. I told Annita our story, and since you know about us, I'll tell it to you, as well."

"You would trust me with that?"

"I would."

Emilios touched his hand to his chest and bowed his head. "I would be honored."

An hour later, Emilios blinked and sat forward in his chair before running a hand down his face. "Thank you for helping my ancestors. I'm sorry we fought."

"You and I didna fight in a war. That was a long time ago, with different people."

"I'd like to say that wouldn't happen now, but I can't," Emilios said with a frown.

Royden waved away his words. "We've come to terms with things. Know that if Annita chooses to be mine, the safest place for her is Dreagan."

"And I want you to know that your secrets are safe with me. I'll go to my grave with them." Emilios got to his feet and held out his hand. "You're a good man."

Royden stood and clasped hands with Emilio. "So are you."

They shared a smile before Emilios turned and walked out of the room leaving Royden with a lot to think over. He sat on the balcony and watched the sun slowly sink into the horizon and darkness blanket the sky. The moon made its ascent, while the stars appeared one by one to wink down at him.

He didn't move from his spot as the blanket was pulled back, and light once more broke on the horizon. The sun was blinding as it chased away the stars. An hour before he was to meet Annita, he rose and used magic to pack up his remaining clothes and send them to Dreagan. Then he checked out of the hotel and paid for his room and had the Vespa returned to the rental shop.

He made his way down to the beach. In a hidden alcove, he stripped bare and began the swim to the cave. Excitement drummed through him as he surfaced in the cave, half expecting to see Annita. But there was still much of the hour left before noon.

Royden got out of the water and made himself comfortable as he waited. Noon came and went without any sign of Annita. Yet, he remained.

For another full day, he stayed in the caves, hoping against hope that Annita would come to him. But as the sun sank the next day, he had to accept the truth. She wasn't coming. She hadn't chosen him. He would be the only Dragon King who had found his mate and didn't return to Dreagan with her.

Royden felt such sadness in his heart that he knew he'd never get over it. He got into the water as the sun set and shifted into his true form, headed toward Dreagan.

Chapter Fourteen

Con was waiting for Royden when he arrived. Royden swooped into Dreagan Mountain and landed. He shifted into human form as Con tossed him a pair of jeans.

"Glad to have you back," the King of Dragon Kings said.

Royden didn't put on the jeans as he looked into Con's black eyes. "I need some time to myself."

"How much time?"

"I'm no' sure."

"I've no' heard from you in a week, but based on your expression, things didna go well."

Royden had heard Con's voice in his head on his swim to Scotland. Even when Royden reached the isle, and he'd used the cover of night to fly home, he still hadn't answered Con. He'd wanted that time to himself. "Nay."

Con crossed his arms over his chest. "What of the prophecy that caused you to remain?"

"A Greek woman was a Seer. Long ago, her ancestors found the talon my brother had taken from me and buried. They sold it and became rich because of it. Chara, the Seer, knew I'd return for the claw. She also knew I was a Dragon King. Her great-niece, Annita, is the one she predicted would find me."

"And Annita did."

Royden nodded. "She did. Chara then told Annita's father the rest of the prophecy."

Con quirked a blond brow. "I'm all ears."

"Chara said Annita was my mate, and that if she chose me, we would strengthen ourselves in an upcoming war—which I suspect is against the Others."

"Most likely. And Annita?"

Royden threw the jeans back at Con. "She isna with me. There's your answer."

"Hmm. You do need your time. Go to your mountain. If things get dire, I'll call for you."

"Thank you."

"Are you sure you doona want to come into the manor first? Maybe try to win Annita's heart?"

Royden shook his head, eager to get to his mountain. "She loves me, but she can no' get past no' having children or seeing her family. I gave her a week to think about things and give me an answer. She was supposed to meet me in the cave, but she didna show up."

Con's lips parted, but Royden was done listening. He shifted and turned before running toward the entrance and jumping into the air, spreading his wings to catch an air current. Con could demand that he return, but Royden hoped he didn't. As the mountain and manor disappeared behind him, Royden locked his gaze on his mountain and flew there as fast as he could.

He breathed a sigh of relief when he reached it. This had been his sanctuary when their world had fallen apart. It would be his refuge once again, though he knew he'd never get over the loss of his mate.

Royden folded his wings and walked through the tunnel to his cavern. He sighed as he lay down and closed his eyes. But try as he might, the dragon sleep he wanted wouldn't come to him.

Chapter Fifteen

There were dragons everywhere. In every room Annita was taken to, she found dragons in pictures, carvings, statues, and metalwork. How could anyone who came to Dreagan not realize who lived there?

The door to Royden's room opened. She turned with a smile on her face, but it wasn't Royden who stood there—it was Con.

Annita searched Con's black eyes. When she arrived two days ago, she'd been more than a little scared. After she told one of the women in the distillery shop who she was and stated that she wanted to speak to Con, she had quickly been ushered into the manor to come face-to-face with the King of Dragon Kings.

He was everything she'd imagined Constantine to be. Imposing, larger-than-life, formidable, and commanding. Yet, he had welcomed her. There hadn't been a smile on his face, at least not at first. She had told him everything, including the rest of the prophecy her father had told her when she chose Royden. Con had listened to it all raptly, and only had one question.

"Why are you no' meeting Royden in the cave as he asked?"

Annita shook her head. "I don't know, really. Something told me to come here."

"An inner voice?"

"Something like that. A feeling, really. A rather persistent one."

Con had smiled then. "I've had such feelings before. It came from the magic of this realm. And it doesna like to be ignored."

"Royden is going to be upset that I wasn't at the cave, isn't he?"

"He'll forget all about it once he sees you."

After that, Con had taken her for a tour of the estate and

introduced her to many people. Then, she'd waited. Just a few hours ago, Con had told her that Royden would be here soon. The fact that he wasn't with Con now wasn't good news.

"He doesn't want to see me," Annita said.

Con walked into the room and closed the door behind him. "Royden isna listening to anyone right now. I could've forced him here, but he's hurting. I think you should go to him."

"You think that's a good idea?"

"Annita, you're his mate. You're the only one he'll listen to right now, unless I issue an order. I doona want to do that," Con said with a smile. "You came here for him. I doona know why the magic brought you here. Perhaps it was to see him in his mountain. We've all suffered in various ways, but I know Royden still carries a lot of guilt. I think you can help with that."

She swallowed and glanced out the window. "Which one is his?"

"I'll take you there."

Instead of walking out the door, Con held out his hand. Annita hesitated just a moment before she took it.

"Hang on," Con said right before he touched a silver cuff on his wrist.

The next instant, the world turned all around her. Annita gasped, then gagged, squeezing her eyes closed.

Con grabbed hold of her to steady her. "Breathe. It's over."

Over? What the hell did that mean? When Annita opened her eyes, she realized they were outside. The nausea passed, and she swiveled her head to look around her. "How did we get here?"

"Magic," Con said with a smile. He jerked his chin to the mountain before them. "This is Royden's. The entrance is there." He pointed. "Follow the tunnel until you find him."

Annita put her hand on his arm before he left. "Thank you. For welcoming me, for believing me, and for this."

"I want my Kings happy."

"And you? What of your happiness?"

He looked away for a heartbeat, a breeze ruffling his wavy, blond hair. "Doona keep Royden waiting."

And then Con was gone. Annita took a deep breath and looked at the mountain. It was dark outside, the moon shedding enough light that she could see the entrance Con had pointed out. She pulled out her mobile and turned on the light to guide.

Once in the mountain, she walked through the tunnel that reminded her a lot of the one Royden had taken her to underwater. She could hear nothing but silence in the mountain. She couldn't be sure Royden was even there. There were no caverns for her to investigate, just the massive tunnel that would be big enough for Royden to walk through in his true form.

Then, suddenly, the tunnel opened into a cavern. She halted, her gaze locked on Royden as he sat on a boulder with his back to her. He was in mortal form with his head in his hands. She wished she'd ignored whatever had told her to come here and had met him in the cave instead. She never wanted to hurt him this way.

Annita was trying to decide if she should call his name or go to him when Royden's head jerked up. Slowly, he turned around and looked at her. She gave him a smile and started toward him.

"I'm sorry I wasn't at the cave. I've been here," she explained. "Con thinks it was the magic that brought me here. I'm not sure. I thought it would be a nice surprise, but now I see it was the wrong thing to do."

"Nay. As far as I know, the magic has never pulled a mate to Dreagan before. The fact you heard the magic is…amazing."

She halted and swallowed. "My father told me everything after I'd made my decision to choose you. I love you."

Royden jumped down from the rock. "Nay, it wasna the wrong thing to do to come here."

"Really?" Relief surged through her as she smiled. "I was waiting for you in your room."

He strode to her and yanked her against him, holding her so tightly she could barely breathe. "I thought I'd lost you."

"I was always meant to be yours," she said and kissed the side of his neck.

He pulled back and looked at her. "I love you."

"And I love you."

"We'll see your family as much as we can."

She put a finger to his lips. "I know we will. I can talk to them often, too. As for children, what happens, happens. If it's meant to be, then we'll have them. If it isn't, then it isn't."

"I doona know what I ever did to deserve you, but I'm so glad you chose me."

Annita sighed in contentment as she smiled up at him. "And I'm glad you chose me, my Dragon King."

Epilogue

Two weeks later...

Royden hadn't thought he could get any happier. Yet every day Annita was in his arms as dawn broke, he found himself more and more delighted. He squeezed her tightly and kissed her temple.

"Hmm. Good morning," she said in a sleepy voice.

"Morning."

She lifted her head from his chest and looked at him. "Are you ready to leave Dreagan today?"

Royden chuckled and rolled her onto her back. "You say that as if we're going to war."

"To some people, going to see their future in-laws is exactly that."

"No' for me."

"I like that you like my family. And I still can't believe you told my father everything."

Royden shrugged. "He already knew so much thanks to your great-aunt. I know he's a man I can trust with our secrets."

"He is," she replied.

"Come on," Royden said as he got off the bed and pulled her after him. "It's time to get dressed."

Annita jumped up but wrapped her arms around his neck and kissed him. "I've told you this before, but I'll keep saying it. I don't care what enemies come out of the woodwork. I'll stand beside you and everyone else here at Dreagan. Always. Whether I'm your mate or not."

"I know," he said as he gazed into her pale brown eyes.

"Good," she said in her sassiest voice before she turned and began to dress.

Royden watched her, thinking about how things were heating up with the Others. He wouldn't change anything with Annita, but that didn't stop his worry about what could happen to her and all of them if the Others won. Which meant they couldn't allow that to happen. No matter what they needed to do, no matter who they needed to align with, the Others would be defeated once and for all.

Annita looked up at him and smiled. He returned it, his heart swelling even more. He had his mate. It wasn't something he'd ever believed would be his, but now that Annita was with him, he'd fight harder than ever before for their future—and the future of all the Dragon Kings and their mates.

A future for every human.

For every dragon.

Because the lines between dragons and humans were blurring more and more as the years passed. And that might not be a bad thing.

* * * *

Also from 1001 Dark Nights and Donna Grant, discover Dragon Claimed, Dragon Night, Dragon King, Dragon Fever, and Dragon Burn.

Sign up for the 1001 Dark Nights Newsletter
and be entered to win a Tiffany Key necklace.

There's a contest every month!

Go to www.1001DarkNights.com to subscribe.

**As a bonus, all subscribers can download
FIVE FREE exclusive books!**

Discover 1001 Dark Nights Collection Seven

For more information, go to www.1001DarkNights.com.

THE BISHOP by Skye Warren
A Tanglewood Novella

TAKEN WITH YOU by Carrie Ann Ryan
A Fractured Connections Novella

DRAGON LOST by Donna Grant
A Dark Kings Novella

SEXY LOVE by Carly Phillips
A Sexy Series Novella

PROVOKE by Rachel Van Dyken
A Seaside Pictures Novella

RAFE by Sawyer Bennett
An Arizona Vengeance Novella

THE NAUGHTY PRINCESS by Claire Contreras
A Sexy Royals Novella

THE GRAVEYARD SHIFT by Darynda Jones
A Charley Davidson Novella

CHARMED by Lexi Blake
A Masters and Mercenaries Novella

SACRIFICE OF DARKNESS by Alexandra Ivy
A Guardians of Eternity Novella

THE QUEEN by Jen Armentrout
A Wicked Novella

BEGIN AGAIN by Jennifer Probst
A Stay Novella

VIXEN by Rebecca Zanetti
A Dark Protectors/Rebels Novella

SLASH by Laurelin Paige
A Slay Series Novella

THE DEAD HEAT OF SUMMER by Heather Graham
A Krewe of Hunters Novella

WILD FIRE by Kristen Ashley
A Chaos Novella

MORE THAN PROTECT YOU by Shayla Black
A More Than Words Novella

LOVE SONG by Kylie Scott
A Stage Dive Novella

CHERISH ME by J. Kenner
A Stark Ever After Novella

SHINE WITH ME by Kristen Proby
A With Me in Seattle Novella

And new from Blue Box Press:

TEASE ME by J. Kenner
A Stark International Novel

Discover More Donna Grant

Dragon Claimed
A Dark Kings Novella

Born to rule the skies as a Dragon King with power and magic, Cináed hides his true identity in the mountains of Scotland with the rest of his brethren. But there is no respite for them as they protect the planet and the human occupants from threats. However, a new, more dangerous enemy has targeted the Kings. One that will stop at nothing until dragons are gone forever. But Cináed discovers a woman from a powerful, ancient Druid bloodline who might have a connection to this new foe.

Solitude is sanctuary for Gemma. Her young life was upended one stormy night when her family disappears, leaving her utterly alone. She learned to depend solely on herself from then on. But no matter where she goes she feels…lost. As if she missed the path she was supposed to take. Everything changes when she backs into the most dangerously seductive man she's ever laid eyes. Gemma surrenders to the all-consuming attraction and the wild, impossible love that could destroy them both – and finds her path amid magic and dragons.

* * * *

Dragon Night
A Dark Kings Novella

Governed by honor and ruled by desire

There has never been a hunt that Dorian has lost. With his sights sent on a relic the Dragon Kings need to battle an ancient foe, he won't let anything stand in his way – especially not the beautiful owner. Alexandra is smart and cautious. Yet the attraction between them is impossible to deny – or ignore. But is it a road Dorian dares to travel down again?

With her vast family fortune, Alexandra Sheridan is never without suitors. No one is more surprised than she when the charming, devilish Scotsman snags her attention. But the secrets Dorian holds is like a wall between them until one fateful night when he shares everything. In his arms she finds passion like no other – and a love that will transcend time. But can she give her heart to a dragon??

* * * *

Dragon Burn
A Dark Kings Novella

In this scorching Dark Kings novella, *New York Times* bestselling author Donna Grant brings together a determined Dragon King used to getting what he wants and an Ice Queen who thaws for no one.

Marked by passion
A promise made eons ago sends Sebastian to Italy on the hunt to find an enemy. His quarry proves difficult to locate, but there is someone who can point him in the right direction – a woman as frigid as the north. Using every seductive skill he's acquired over his immortal life, his seduction begins. Until he discovers that the passion he stirs within her makes him burn for more…

Gianna Santini has one love in her life – work. A disastrous failed marriage was evidence enough to realize she was better off on her own. That is until a handsome Scot strolled into her life and literally swept her off her feet. She is unprepared for the blazing passion between them or the truth he exposes. But as her world begins to unravel, she realizes the only one she can depend on is the very one destroying everything - a Dragon King.

* * * *

Dragon Fever
A Dark Kings Novella

A yearning that won't be denied
Rachel Marek is a journalist with a plan. She intends to expose the truth about dragons to the world – and her target is within sight. Nothing matters but getting the truth, especially not the ruggedly handsome, roguishly thrilling Highlander who oozes danger and charm. And when she finds the truth that shatters her faith, she'll have to trust her heart to the very man who can crush it…

A legend in the flesh

Suave, dashing Asher is more than just a man. He's a Dragon King – a being who has roamed this planet since the beginning of time. With everything on the line, Asher must choose to trust an enemy in the form of an all too alluring woman whose tenacity and passion captivate him. Together, Asher and Rachel must fight for their lives – and their love – before an old enemy destroys them both…

* * * *

Dragon King
A Dark Kings Novella

A Woman On A Mission

Grace Clark has always done things safe. She's never colored outside of the law, but she has a book due and has found the perfect spot to break through her writer's block. Or so she thinks. Right up until Arian suddenly appears and tries to force her away from the mountain. Unaware of the war she just stumbled into, Grace doesn't just discover the perfect place to write, she finds Arian - the most gorgeous, enticing, mysterious man she's ever met.

A King With a Purpose

Arian is a Dragon King who has slept away centuries in his cave. Recently woken, he's about to leave his mountain to join his brethren in a war when he's alerted that someone has crossed onto Dreagan. He's ready to fight...until he sees the woman. She's innocent and mortal - and she sets his blood aflame. He recognizes the danger approaching her just as the dragon within him demands he claim her for his own...

Dragon Claimed

By Donna Grant

A Dark Kings Novella

Born to rule the skies as a Dragon King with power and magic, Cináed hides his true identity in the mountains of Scotland with the rest of his brethren. But there is no respite for them as they protect the planet and the human occupants from threats. However, a new, more dangerous enemy has targeted the Kings. One that will stop at nothing until dragons are gone forever. But Cináed discovers a woman from a powerful, ancient Druid bloodline who might have a connection to this new foe.

Solitude is sanctuary for Gemma. Her young life was upended one stormy night when her family disappears, leaving her utterly alone. She learned to depend solely on herself from then on. But no matter where she goes she feels…lost. As if she missed the path she was supposed to take. Everything changes when she backs into the most dangerously seductive man she's ever laid eyes. Gemma surrenders to the all-consuming attraction and the wild, impossible love that could destroy them both – and finds her path amid magic and dragons.

* * * *

Present Day
Dreagan

Cináed rubbed his eyes and sat back in the chair. He should have known better than to tell Ryder he was willing to help out. Cináed thought he might get to use his skills on the computer.

Instead, Ryder had him looking through old newspapers from all over Scotland in search of anything out of the ordinary. It began three weeks ago, and Cináed made his way through one huge stack only to be told that was from Glasgow. Then he was shown other stacks.

It would help if Ryder had some idea what he wanted him to look for, but all Cináed got in reply was that if it sounded odd, put it aside.

Humans reported on every little thing. Cináed actually thought he wouldn't find many odd things in the newspaper, but he'd been wrong. More often than not, he was setting aside a paper to show Ryder.

Cináed popped the last raspberry biscuit in his mouth and reached for the next paper. He was now on the newspapers from Inverness, and finding quite a bit that was 'odd.'

He propped his foot up on the stool before him while reading about a reporter's take on the queen's recent visit to Balmoral Castle. Cináed fought to stay awake. He kept yawning as he moved from story to story with nothing catching his eye.

It was on the third page of the newspaper on the bottom right-hand side that he spotted the headline: **Young Girl Found Alone on Isle**.

Below it was a close-up picture of a pretty child with her head turned staring into the camera. The black and white photo didn't show the color of the lass's long hair that had tendrils flying across her face from the wind.

There was something in the girl's eyes that wouldn't let him look away. Misery, despair, and acceptance stared back at him from the picture.

It was several minutes before Cináed read the article about how the girl—a Gemma Atherton—was found alone. The isle had been purchased by a Mr. Ben Sinclair ten years prior. With three houses and a tiny post office, the isle only held a family of four. Presumably the girl's family.

Cináed was surprised to read that Gemma had no idea where her family had gone. The article went on to say that there was a search for the mother, father, and son across the United Kingdom, the surrounding isles, as well as the seas.

A family going missing certainly constituted something odd. Cináed put the paper aside to show Ryder later, but he soon picked it back up again. He read the article three more times. And each instance he wondered what had become of the girl and if her family had been found.

Cináed folded the newspaper so that the article was on top and picked up the rest of the oddities he'd found that day before he stood and made his way to the computer room, which was Ryder's domain.

He met Kinsey on the stairs. Ryder's mate had a box of donuts in hand as she smiled at him. He didn't need to ask if every pastry in there was jelly-filled, because those were Ryder's favorites.

"You found something," Kinsey said.

He looked into her violet eyes and shrugged. "Maybe."

"Anything you want me to look into?"

"Actually, I'd like to look myself."

Her dark brows shot up on her forehead. "I see."

They reached the door to the computer room. Cináed opened it and waited for Kinsey to enter before he followed. Ryder didn't glance away from the multiple rows of screens he watched. Instead, he held out his hand, waiting for Kinsey to take it when she walked to him. After they shared a quick kiss, she sat in the chair next to him and set the box of donuts down.

"More things for me to look into?" Ryder asked him.

Cináed set the papers on Ryder's desk but kept the top one. That got Ryder's attention. He pulled his hands away from the keyboard and focused on Cináed.

"What did you find?" Ryder asked.

Every Dragon King had their own special magic. Guy could take away someone's memories. Constantine could heal anything but death. Ulrik could bring someone back from the dead—or obliterate their soul. Kiril could freeze anything.

And the list went on and on.

For Ryder, he could make and operate anything electronic. Computers were his specialty. There wasn't a hacker in the world who could get through his firewalls. And there was no security system in operation that could keep him out.

If anyone needed anything looked for at Dreagan, they went to Ryder. With his facial recognition software, and the ability to search the entire world for a needle, he got the job done quickly.

Cináed's ability wasn't so cut and dry. When he wanted to learn something, he was able to do it. Whatever that might be. For a while he'd helped Vaughn with his legal practice, but Cináed was ready to move on to something else. He'd now turned to computers, which Ryder had been happy to show him.

Ryder slowly smiled. "Something caught your attention."

"Aye," Cináed said.

Ryder then pointed to one of the other keyboards. "Get on it."

Cináed walked to the chair. Before he reached it, Ryder had turned control of the screen to him. He sat and popped his knuckles as he glanced at the photo of the girl once more. Gemma Atherton.

What was it about that name that caused him to frown? He should know that name. Maybe he'd find out when he discovered what had happened to the child.

Cináed opened up a search page. He then typed in the girl's name and "missing family" before he hit enter. Instantly the screen was filled with links. One by one he went through them reading what was said. He highlighted anything he found important before moving onto the next.

It wasn't long before he was utterly absorbed in his search. Gemma had dominated the headlines across the UK for several months. There were many pictures of her, but in every one she had the same expression from the first photo.

Then, suddenly, there were no new pictures. The papers re-used photos. As odd as Cináed found that, what was more puzzling was that the authorities had found nothing of her parents or brother.

After a few months, Gemma's name stopped being printed as the talk centered on the missing parents and son. There was a search of the isle for bodies, which made him roll his eyes. As if Gemma had murdered her family. Anyone in their right mind could look at her and know a seven-year-old didn't do it.

Cináed frowned. This happened years ago, but he still was sure of her innocence. He finished the article and went on to the next, but there was nothing. Everything about Gemma Atherton and her family ceased.

Another search to find what had happened to Gemma netted him nothing. But Cináed had been taught by Ryder, so he wasn't deterred. His next search gave him exactly what he wanted.

Gemma had become a ward of the state and gone into foster care. He was able to bypass the security from the government and get into the files. There he discovered that Gemma's foster parents had put her into therapy to talk about what had happened, but after seven different therapists over a three-year period, everyone came to realize that she wasn't going to discuss it.

Gemma kept to herself, shying away from others. She made decent grades and finished school. As soon as she came of age, she left her foster parents' home. The documents from the government ended as well.

But Cináed knew there was more. It took some digging, and a couple of tries remembering what Ryder had taught him, but he found what he was looking for on social media using the facial recognition software.

The one final picture of Gemma in the files when she came of age made it easy to pop that into the software and search the entire Internet for her. Unfortunately, it was a search that would take hours.

Cináed pushed back the chair and ran a hand down his face. He didn't understand the connection he felt to Gemma, but it was there.

Maybe he just felt sorry for her that her family disappeared.

He spun the office chair as he was about to stand, but he spotted Ryder leaned back in his own chair, legs stretched out and ankles crossed as he watched Cináed.

"You've been glued to the screen for twelve hours," Ryder said.

Cináed frowned and looked at the time. It had been twelve hours. He shrugged and swung his gaze back to Ryder. "There was a lot to look through."

"Who is Gemma Atherton?"

"I don't know."

Ryder quirked a blond brow. "She obviously intrigued you."

"I found this," Cináed said and tossed him the article. "That seven-year-old's parents and older brother disappeared one night. She wouldn't say how long she was on that isle by herself with her dog, but my guess is awhile."

"Maybe her family meant to leave her."

"Hmm. I think it's more than that. Something isna adding up."

"If I know the authorities, they took pictures of everything. Did you look at those?"

Damn. Cináed knew there had been something he was missing. He slid around as Ryder sat up and swiveled his chair to start typing. Within seconds, the pictures filled two of the many screens.

Ryder clicked on each one, letting it fill an entire screen so they could get a closer look. It didn't take long for Cináed to realize that this was no cut-and-dried case.

"Would a woman leave something that is obviously an antique behind?" Cináed asked as he pointed to the broach in one of the pictures.

Ryder shook his head. "I doona think so. No' on purpose, at least. Look at the bedrooms."

Cináed inspected each one. "They're messy. Drawers half opened. In all except this one," he said, pointing to what was obviously Gemma's room.

"I suppose the parents could have tried to get away without her knowing."

"On an isle with no one else about? And Gemma had a dog."

Ryder's lips twisted. "I forgot about the dog."

"The only way on or off the isle was by water. Is there a boat in Ben Sinclair's name?"

"Is he the father?" Ryder asked as he typed in the name.

"That's the name listed as the owner of the isle."

Ryder grunted. "That's odd."

"What is?"

"There are many Ben Sinclairs, but none of them are the one who purchased the isle."

Cináed turned to Kinsey's computer since she wasn't there and began digging into the name. Between him and Ryder, it didn't take long for them to discover that Ben Sinclair wasn't a real person. Through several shell companies, the isle was in fact purchased by a Daniel Atherton.

"The father," Cináed said with a frown.

"There is a boat in the name of Ben Sinclair as well."

"Why did he buy both under a fake name?"

"No one does that unless they're hiding from something. Or someone."

Cináed recalled something he'd read in one of the papers. He did another hunt and found there was a storm that had hit the west coast of Scotland three weeks before Gemma was found.

"I'll be damned," Ryder mumbled. "Do you think she fell overboard and managed to get back to the isle?"

Cináed shrugged. "I've no idea, but I'd like to find out."

"Why is this important?"

"I can no' explain it," he said, meeting Ryder's hazel gaze. "I just know I have to find her."

No sooner had the words left his mouth than his computer dinged. He looked at it to discover that the search had finished.

"That was quick," Ryder said with a frown. "Too quick."

Cináed pushed his chair back to the computer and quickly ran through the photos of Gemma. There were only a few, and then nothing for several years. There were more recent ones of her going back about eight years.

"This is why you look for names as well as faces," Ryder said as he tapped his finger on the screen.

Cináed looked to discover that she had changed her name to Gemma Clacher. That was odd enough since that surname was linked to Henry and Esther North, a brother and sister who recently discovered they were adopted and their names changed to hide the fact that they were the JusticeBringer and TruthSeeker of the Druids.

"That has to be a coincidence," Cináed said.

Ryder blew out a breath. "Is it? Or does it mean something else? Look where she's living."

Cináed scanned the screen until he saw it, shock rushing through him. "She's here. Right here in the village."

About Donna Grant

New York Times and *USA Today* bestselling author Donna Grant has been praised for her "totally addictive" and "unique and sensual" stories. Her latest acclaimed series, Dark Kings, features a thrilling combination of dragons, Fae, and immortal Highlanders who are dark, dangerous, and irresistible. She lives with her two children and an assortment of animals in Texas.

Visit Donna at www.DonnaGrant.com
and www.MotherOfDragonsBooks.com

Discover 1001 Dark Nights

COLLECTION THREE
HIDDEN INK by Carrie Ann Ryan
BLOOD ON THE BAYOU by Heather Graham
SEARCHING FOR MINE by Jennifer Probst
DANCE OF DESIRE by Christopher Rice
ROUGH RHYTHM by Tessa Bailey
DEVOTED by Lexi Blake
Z by Larissa Ione
FALLING UNDER YOU by Laurelin Paige
EASY FOR KEEPS by Kristen Proby
UNCHAINED by Elisabeth Naughton
HARD TO SERVE by Laura Kaye
DRAGON FEVER by Donna Grant
KAYDEN/SIMON by Alexandra Ivy/Laura Wright
STRUNG UP by Lorelei James
MIDNIGHT UNTAMED by Lara Adrian
TRICKED by Rebecca Zanetti
DIRTY WICKED by Shayla Black
THE ONLY ONE by Lauren Blakely
SWEET SURRENDER by Liliana Hart

COLLECTION FOUR
ROCK CHICK REAWAKENING by Kristen Ashley
ADORING INK by Carrie Ann Ryan
SWEET RIVALRY by K. Bromberg
SHADE'S LADY by Joanna Wylde
RAZR by Larissa Ione
ARRANGED by Lexi Blake
TANGLED by Rebecca Zanetti
HOLD ME by J. Kenner
SOMEHOW, SOME WAY by Jennifer Probst
TOO CLOSE TO CALL by Tessa Bailey
HUNTED by Elisabeth Naughton
EYES ON YOU by Laura Kaye
BLADE by Alexandra Ivy/Laura Wright
DRAGON BURN by Donna Grant
TRIPPED OUT by Lorelei James
STUD FINDER by Lauren Blakely
MIDNIGHT UNLEASHED by Lara Adrian

ENCHANTED by Lexi Blake
TAKE THE BRIDE by Carly Phillips
INDULGE ME by J. Kenner
THE KING by Jennifer L. Armentrout
QUIET MAN by Kristen Ashley
ABANDON by Rachel Van Dyken
THE OPEN DOOR by Laurelin Paige
CLOSER by Kylie Scott
SOMETHING JUST LIKE THIS by Jennifer Probst
BLOOD NIGHT by Heather Graham
TWIST OF FATE by Jill Shalvis
MORE THAN PLEASURE YOU by Shayla Black
WONDER WITH ME by Kristen Proby
THE DARKEST ASSASSIN by Gena Showalter

Discover Blue Box Press

TAME ME by J. Kenner
TEMPT ME by J. Kenner
DAMIEN by J. Kenner
TEASE ME by J. Kenner
REAPER by Larissa Ione
THE SURRENDER GATE by Christopher Rice
SERVICING THE TARGET by Cherise Sinclair

On Behalf of 1001 Dark Nights,

Liz Berry, M.J. Rose, and Jillian Stein would like to thank ~

Steve Berry
Doug Scofield
Benjamin Stein
Kim Guidroz
InkSlinger PR
Dan Slater
Asha Hossain
Chris Graham
Chelle Olson
Kasi Alexander
Jessica Johns
Dylan Stockton
Richard Blake
and Simon Lipskar

Made in the USA
Monee, IL
16 February 2020